MAKE ME DO THINGS

Also by Victoria Redel

Fiction

Where the Road Bottoms Out: Stories
Loverboy
The Border of Truth

Poetry

Already the World
Swoon
Woman Without Umbrella

MAKE ME DO THINGS

stories by

Victoria Redel

FOUR WAY BOOKS

TRIBECA

Bruce Van Dusen, for you

Please direct all inquiries to:
Editorial Office
Four Way Books
POB 535, Village Station
New York, NY 10014
www.fourwaybooks.com

Library of Congress Cataloging-in-Publication Data

Redel, Victoria.
[Short stories. Selections]
Make me do things : stories / by Victoria Redel.
pages ; cm.
ISBN 978-1-935536-37-6 (alk. paper)
I. Redel, Victoria. You look like you do. II. Title.
PS3568.E3443M35 2013
813'.54--dc23

2013010098

This book is manufactured in the United States of America
and printed on acid-free paper.

Four Way Books is a not-for-profit literary press. We are grateful for the assistance
we receive from individual donors, public arts agencies, and private foundations.

NYSCA

This publication is made possible with public funds from
the New York State Council on the Arts, a state agency.

[clmp]

We are a proud member
of the Council of Literary Magazines and Presses.

Distributed by University Press of New England
One Court Street, Lebanon, NH 03766

TABLE OF CONTENTS

YOU LOOK LIKE YOU DO

IT WAS THERE, LATE INTO THE PARTY, AFTER THE BIRTHDAY CAKE HAD been served, after she'd drunk a good deal of red wine and taken too many hits from the joints that floated by her, that the husband told Sabina that he and his wife had been thinking about her, that they'd both been thinking about her since that first night they'd met her a few weeks back. "When we're making love," he said, "we think about you all the time," and he leaned close to her then and asked would she stay after everyone else had left.

"Why are you thinking about me?" She laughed, tilting her head over to the wife. The wife was talking with another woman near a table arrayed in empty wine bottles. Both women swayed to the party music. Marley, the wife, was young, not yet even thirty, with long, honey hair and a body so slender that sometimes, like this night, she looked like a teenager, a Dutch au pair, instead of the mother of twin girls who had fallen asleep in their double stroller and, like angels, stayed asleep even when the music was cranked and the guests danced.

"We are," the man said gently. "I can only tell you that we are."

"That's crazy." Sabina twirled at her short hair. "Are you looking at what you've got right over there?"

"Isn't it crazy?" she told Teddy. This morning he had her doing super-sets—lunges and dips, then side squats and bench presses. They worked in a quiet part of the gym.

"You've been locked up with kids for too long, girl," he said. "Welcome to the world."

Teddy was at least a little right about parenting—a lock-up or -down—it was nights of homework, dinner, homework, dinner, Code-Orange meltdowns and exhausted mornings when Sabina was somehow to blame when a kid's shoe was MIA.

Then Teddy told her about a man who'd approached him once, offering any amount of money Teddy could name to fuck this guy's drop-dead fucking gorgeous wife, any you-name-it-amount for the guy to watch Teddy go to it with his wife.

"Come on, wasn't that a movie plot? Did you do it?" Sabina asked, stepping out on her second set of lunges. On the return, she stopped in front of the mirror for bicep curls. "What's he want with me?" she asked.

"I'm saying it's pretty obvious what he wants." Teddy motioned for her final set, flicking the back of her legs with a towel. "You think all this work here is going for nothing?"

Why are you wasting this toned-up body? Teddy had been saying for the last year. He'd been right about the squats and banishing white flour. And now after her second time saying yes to an invite, Sabina wasn't going on about her son's math grade; she had a wild story that practically matched his.

"Well, I'm just saying, this guy's wife is practically too young for you, Romeo," she said and handed Teddy the twelve-pound weights.

The husband, Antonio, was from Barcelona, saying everything with a soft carpety *th* sound. He was slight and fair-skinned, which didn't fit Sabina's rugged image of a Spaniard. He was older than Marley by more than twenty years, and though he swore he'd never wanted children, now he couldn't stop extolling his good fortune. He cha-chaed close to the stroller. "It's good they're so damn cute," he crooned over and over with a delight that his wife called to the guests' attention.

"Listen to what Antonio's become." Marley tried to sound annoyed but to Sabina it sounded like crooning.

As a rule, if Sabina ever even went to parties, she left them early. Even if her kids were sleeping out, she could say, "I've got to get home and make sure someone keeps to a curfew in our family." But last night Sabina had stayed late—she hadn't even noticed how late until the party thinned to this last seven or eight and they'd all drifted back into dancing. Sabina danced salsa with a man named Tomaso. He'd paid attention to Sabina all evening, but even still, Sabina was pretty sure from the two-toned suede shoes he had to be gay. She could see Antonio and Marley as they danced. They were both small and blond and they fit together just right, his leg locked between hers. Their moves were practiced but not show-offy. Sabina could see his mouth moving, whispering against Marley's cheek.

"You're strict," Sabina said to Tomaso, who kept pulling her in, correcting her position. There was a flirty tone in her voice that was new. She wasn't sure what to make of it. But it was all new. When was the last time she had danced with anyone but her husband or maybe a few other people's husbands at weddings? Tomaso adjusted her stance, pressing her elbow up with his. He pushed with his hip and Sabina stepped back.

"Am I learning fast enough?" Sabina tried to keep eye contact with Tomaso. His shaved head looked oiled. "I've got you," Tomaso said. "Just stop trying to lead." When he pulled her back in from a spin, he pulled her close, cheek to cheek. "You smell delicious," he said, keeping her movements tight until the end of the song.

"We're so happy you came to my birthday," Marley said when the dancing ended and Sabina and the last stragglers lingered in the tight vestibule. "I don't want my night with you to end." She kissed Sabina on both cheeks. She sounded excited and overtired, like a kid at the end of a birthday party. Sabina was sure she didn't mean it the way Antonio had meant it.

"Tomaso, you'll get my new best friend home safely," Marley said and buttoned the top button of Sabina's coat.

"I'm fine, really," Sabina said to Tomaso, but then she heard her voice soften, "if you'd just help me into a cab."

It was a strange secret she carried around all week. Not that she thought about them during meetings at work, but wiping down the counter after dinner, or now, sitting in the bleachers at her son's basketball game, she looked around at the other moms in their jeans and cardigan sweaters, their extravagant, large purses junked beside cashmere coats, their dutiful shouts of "Defense! Defense!" and thought about Antonio and Marley. She wasn't conjuring anything explicit. She couldn't really figure that out exactly, the abundance of limbs and parts didn't even seem very appealing, but it felt sexy; it made her feel sexy. She felt excited, complicit. She wasn't going to do anything, but she felt somehow like she had already done it.

"You're dating?" a mother of a boy on the team asked, though it sounded more like she had discovered Sabina in flagrante delicto. Sabina had known this mom since the boys were in grade school. But right now she was spacing on her name—an *S* name, she knew that— it would come to her. They'd helped at the school carnival together, painting Spider-Man and Little Mermaid faces at the makeup booth. This woman—Sheila, that was it!—had been kinder than many during the divorce.

"Nothing really serious," Sabina said. She hoped the conversation could end there. Sabina hadn't gone on anything resembling a date in more than a year.

"Perfect," Sheila said. "I could go for a lot of nights with Mr. Nothing Serious." The two women laughed. A whistle blew and the women turned to the court. The coach was out on the court, arguing with the referee. "And let me start with this Mr. Hot Temper." Sabina could have sworn she heard Sheila growl.

Sabina tried to see him as something hot but he looked just out of college, wearing the same permanent-press dress shirt and tie at every game, where he was in constant motion, running up and down, pointing and jabbing his finger in the air between him and the referee.

"Please Sheila, do us a favor and tire him out so our boys actually have a chance to play ball." Sabina said.

"I'm just saying, with two kids practically out the door, I definitely wouldn't be rushing into the marriage thing."

Sabina liked Sheila and her husband. They were a good couple, one of the rock-solid as far as Sabina could assess, although she knew the obvious—that whatever you think you know, you don't know jackshit about anyone else's marriage. Still, she thought she could tell which marriages had some oomph left in them and which ones were basically kaput.

But now there was this whole private world in marriage she'd never thought about. Did Sheila and her husband whisper smutty fantasies to one another? Did she tell her husband that she imagined fucking their son's basketball coach? Did her husband ask her to pretend to be the airline attendant he'd flirted with, coming home from Detroit?

Sabina and her husband had never spun fantasies. She didn't

think she'd really had any fantasies. "We fit together real good, like a special order," her husband liked to say sometimes after making love, and Sabina would press her face down against the familiar smell of his chest, saying, "I don't think it gets better than this." Like that, they'd had a perfectly good time together—until they weren't having a perfectly good time, and then when it was over, everything so unwound around them that they tripped just getting from the bed to the bathroom, where they both looked at each other with dazed sorrow. They seemed more confused than anything else when they spoke on the phone or sat next to one another at one of the kids' games or concerts.

Now Sabina wondered if they'd been narrow-minded, relying on their bodies' limited resources. Maybe if they'd been the kind of people who came up with games, who brought toys—maybe even other bodies—into bed with them, it would have been healthy, like a weekend getaway, a way of letting some fresh country air into the marriage.

Sabina's son scored the last three-pointer and all the parents were up in the stands shouting. Sabina was on her feet. The other team was only up by a point.

"That's it, Stevie. Give us another one! Go Stevie!" Sheila was shouting Sabina's boy's name, and adding that cutesy end onto "Steve." Sabina never shouted at the games. She didn't want to look like one of those out-of-control parents or the embarrassing mom that shouted, "Go, my baby!" Steve had even assured her, "If you become one of the mother shouters, you're banished."

Steve intercepted the ball and drove it down the court. Arms lifted, Sabina clenched her fists Black Panther style, punching just the slightest with each Go! Go! Go! Go! she shouted robustly in her head.

"You absolutely must be dating," Sheila said when they sat on the bleachers. "You have quite a new look happening, I'm happy for you."

Something was definitely happening. But fuck if Sabina knew what it was. Walking down the street in dreary mid-February cold, wrapped in her coat and scarf, Sabina could see she was getting noticed. Men— young, old, white, black, Latino—were checking her out, some saying hello, even a bold "You're so hot."

Suddenly I'm *hot*? Sabina laughed for a block. But it felt true, at least a little true. Her walk had shifted, not a sashay or anything ridiculous, but Sabina felt a line running through her—maybe it was all just Teddy's work on core strength—her carriage was up, a bit thrown back. She took quick looks at herself in storefronts.

She crossed in front of a guy who held open the coffee-shop door. "My pleasure," he said when Sabina nodded thanks. The guy was wearing a parka, shorts and flip-flops, and had a thick ring plugged through his nose.

"You're not freezing?" Sabina never talked to strangers, but— hello!—now she was talking to guys with piercings.

"Not anymore," he bowed slightly as she passed. "Come on, Sunshine, you make it summertime."

"Jesus, Mom. You have a busier life than me," Sabina's daughter teased. "What are you, the gay divorcée?"

"I might be." Sabina was at the stove, getting dinner ready for the kids. Her high heels clicked on the floor tiles as she moved between the stove and sink to drain the ravioli. It was true: after two years on the sofa, Sabina was now up and dressing for a continuous calender of dinners and birthdays. By early spring, it seemed Sabina had become part of some ongoing world party: Spaniards, Italians, Latin Americans, everyone had another home somewhere else, and Sabina kept getting offers for vacations. There was always a book party for a new friend's novel or cocktails for someone's ex-wife who'd arrived from Costa Brava. She hadn't danced this much since college.

"Do you have a boyfriend?" Her daughter looked hard at her mother.

Sabina put a clump of pesto in a bowl and began to toss. "No, honey," she said. "It's all a lot more boring. No boyfriend."

"Well, you look like you do," her daughter accused.

Another intimate dinner. Marley, legs tucked under her, squirreled close to Sabina on a low couch. "I'm so glad to see you," Marley said in a velvety whisper. She reached out and stroked Sabina's short hair. It seemed like something Sabina's daughter and her friends did, something they'd picked up from the music videos the kids watched until they blasted out of Sabina's house, claiming they were heading to another kid's house.

"I'm glad to see you, too," Sabina said. Her voice sounded formal and she tried to adjust it. "How are the twins?"

"Delicious," Marley said, "and most delicious when they're asleep." They both laughed. It felt good to laugh with her about mother stuff, normal stuff, things Sabina was comfortable speaking about, had spoken about for years.

But later in the night, there was Antonio saying, "You look amazing. I loved watching you across the room when you were talking with my wife." His hand slid along the length of Sabina's torso. "Marvelous," he said, and his eyes went a little swimmy.

And later still, he motioned to Sabina, and when she came over, he asked her to sit with them on the couch. "We missed you," he said. Sabina looked at Marley, trying to read whether she had any idea what Antonio had said to her, but Marley's eyes were closed.

Sabina thought she should turn and find someone to dance with. Where was Tomaso?

"Please," said Marley, her eyes still closed, reaching out a hand for Sabina.

"I think it's really time for me to get home." Sabina let Marley pull her down. Marley kept hold of Sabina's hand, letting her arm relax against Sabina's leg. Marley's arm was smooth, impossibly tiny-wristed, with no hair at all. Antonio reached his hand across and put his hand on the women's hands. It looked like the hand pileup her son and his teammates did before a game.

"My wife is too amazing," Antonio said and kissed Marley on the lips. He drew back and looked directly at Sabina and went into the kiss again. Marley's hand tightened and then relaxed, and when it tightened again, Antonio had worked his hand between the two women's. Sabina knew he was kissing Marley for her attention, but still she felt trapped, like the odd girl out at a middle-school party where the mood has shifted from Twister to Seven Minutes in Heaven.

Or worse, in college, where she had once listened to her room-mate and a boyfriend endlessly screw in the bunk below. She couldn't believe something could go on quite so long, the flimsy metal frame jostling, the two of them below her breathing and laughing and actually grunting till finally her roommate squealed, "Sabina, I'm sorry!" When she said it again in the morning, Sabina pretended she'd slept through it all. But now, with Antonio and Marley kissing and the hands doing some pressing, grabby thing in her lap, she couldn't fake sleep—and then she felt another hand, Antonio's, drawing a slow, repeating line up to her ear and back down the length of her neck.

Sabina looked around to see if anyone had taken notice of the three of them, but the clusters of conversation were dense and sparkly. No one was looking. And what was there to see? A husband and wife kissing, what was the big deal? Maybe it was no big deal, really, all an exaggerated Spanish way of speaking, just a little thrilling Spanish affection; clearly Antonio and Marley were mad for one another. Even Antonio's hand on her neck was just affection, a friendly thing, and, face it, it felt good. Sabina decided she could stand being a little less American.

"You really think you know what's American? I'll tell you about American." Teddy stood behind Sabina, spotting her on the bench press. He'd put extra weights on, claiming she better step up into the big time.

Sabina lowered the bar, working to bring it down close to her chest before pressing up.

"Take a look at me. Midwestern, football player, black and Native American but growing up in an all-white town, I'm asking, Is there anything more American than me?" Teddy said. "When I went home last Christmas, all my married friends were doing the name-in-the-hat thing."

"What hat thing?" Sabina wrestled the bar into the weight rack.

"That's what I'm talking about, you've been in la-la land, girl. The name-in-the-hat, go-home-with-the-other-guy's-wife thing. It was a kind of seventies revival."

"In Missouri?" Sabina zagged her head to catch if Teddy was bullshitting her.

"They invited me to join in even though I didn't have a wife. I figure I made up for not having a wife by offering black hope. You know, taste black, you can't come back." Teddy busted out a few steps, circling his hips to the beat in the song over the gym speakers.

"Did you?" Sabina wasn't sure what answer she was hoping for.

Teddy took his time, counting out her last set, then dancing his way over to abductor machine.

"I don't roll that way," Teddy said. "Plus, they'd all packed on the big pounds and I definitely wasn't rolling *that* way."

After the parent-teacher conference, Sabina and her ex-husband had their customary coffee, but this time it was Pinot Gris, to celebrate—of course they should—the incredible year their daughter had which, "Let's face it," Sabina said, "it means we didn't screw up too bad, even though we totally screwed up."

They knocked glasses at that. Why not? A good kid. She was a hardworking, straight-A kid, well positioned—even in these insane demographics, these you-have-to-be-in-line-for-a-Nobel-Prize-by-graduation times—to get into the college where Sabina and her ex-husband met and fell in love, though both were certain they'd never be accepted under current conditions. And not only a smarty-pants. The advisor recounted one after another story about their daughter's daily acts of genuine kindness to kids across the board.

But why then, if everything was so okay, did Sabina feel herself start falling from some high perch inside, tumbling down a long, slick, and muddy hillside? She felt she might keep falling until she'd be under the table in a rubbly heap of emotional runoff.

"You seem well," her ex said. She barely thought of him as her ex—even though he had a serious girlfriend who seemed, according to the kids, to be living with him. She thought of him still as her husband, a distant husband, but just because they were divorced, it didn't mean they weren't married. Married with new rules. Mostly better rules. And now that they had been apart for a while, the old hurts and anger had mostly been replaced by fondness, so that the way he swirled and practically gargled the wine seemed sweet rather than pretentious and idiotic.

"I think I am." Sabina took a big sip, hoping the Pinot Gris might steady her when the mudslide started. Her ex looked older. He'd always been so boyish, with his thick, dark hair, his muscular, lean body. For the first time, she could see his hair was thinning. "Things are actually kind of great," she said.

It occurred to Sabina that her ex and his girlfriend might trade fantasies.

His girlfriend was younger than they were by ten years, and had tattoos, a star on her shoulder and a vine thing on her back. Maybe the girlfriend encouraged the new—bringing him into shops where things needed a lot of batteries and everything smelled of overripe fruit.

"Well, something is agreeing with you," he said.

"I guess we have to keep learning new tricks," Sabina said and nodded when the waiter asked if she wanted another glass of wine.

There was something reassuring in imagining her husband, her ex, learning new tricks. Sitting opposite from him, talking about the kids' summer plans, she imagined the girlfriend tying him up and saying rough, degrading things to him. But in her imagination, her husband couldn't stay serious; he kept cracking up and crying, "Uncle, uncle!"

"Sabina, please, please call me back," Tomaso pouted on the second message he left. Sabina assumed there'd be another invitation to another party, but it turned out Tomaso wanted to cook dinner. "There are always so many people. I want a night with you all to myself," he said. "I'm a fabulous cook."

Saturday was fine.

"Promise you'll wear your dancing shoes. Ciao."

Was he planning to give her a lesson? What had he meant by wanting a night with her? She wanted it to be a date. She hadn't been on one in so long that she couldn't figure out the invitation. On the other hand, the use of *fabulous* and *cook* in the same sentence reeked of majorly gay.

But then it was Saturday, and when Tomaso opened the door to his loft, the tinted votive candles positioned all over the room and the open-mouthed kiss at the door seemed to answer the question.

Dinner was pretty *fabulous*. Dinner involved a lot of kissing.

Kissing! Sabina had forgotten just how much she liked kissing! This was the first person beside her husband whose tongue she'd tasted since she was nineteen.

And it was a little like being nineteen again, but better.

"Let's go slowly," Sabina said. She wasn't scared; she just wasn't sure when it would happen again.

"Keep talking," Tomaso said. That threw Sabina. Talk about what? Was it just an encouragement like: *Oh baby, now you're talking—* or was it instructional, like his dance lessons? Sabina tried to work back into the groove, but she was distracted, imagining that soon she'd be expected to narrate like a sportscaster. Everything would have a lot of O's. *I'm sooooo . . . You're sooooo . . .*

"Oh, don't bite," Tomaso pulled back. "Biting? I didn't take you for one of the adventurous girls." He kissed Sabina wetly on the nose.

"Oops," Sabina laughed. A talker. A biter. Now she was an adventurous girl? She wanted to ask if he was okay, had she hurt him, but Tomaso pulled back in, close to Sabina, and was moving his tongue in the lightest, most wonderful circles against her lips, parting her mouth and then teasingly pulling back when her tongue touched his. And then, because she could—because the kids were with her ex, because she better start somewhere, and because she already seemed to be somewhere in the middle, where the kissing had begun to involve their whole bodies working against one another—she went to bed with Tomaso.

It was as though they could smell a change in their mother when the kids came back home on Monday.

"What's with you?" Sabina's daughter said.

Sabina had roasted an organic, free-roaming chicken. There was wild rice and a mesclun salad. Suddenly, the dinner felt less wholesome than promiscuous.

"Stuff," the kids said when she asked about their weekends.

"I'm not your mom." Sabina tried the old joke that used to terrify and delight her children. "I'm the mom imposter. You better check for the telltale scar." She stuck out her hand for the kids to look at the U-shaped scar she'd told them would be her foolproof identification.

"I don't need to look to know you're weird." Sabina's daughter picked over the roasted chicken like it was contaminated.

Teddy told Sabina that over the weekend he'd broken up with the woman from Connecticut.

Sabina tried to remember Connecticut. She remembered Denver, who was in marketing. Boston worked on local television. She thought Connecticut might have been a pilates instructor with a five-year-old. But that might have been Tampa.

"Do long phone conversations really count as dating?" Sabina was on the assisted dips and pull-ups machine. Even assisted, the last pull-ups were hard.

"That's why we broke up. I realized I didn't even want to go on a first date."

She got ready to tell Teddy about the lip-biting and her night with Tomaso but instead she heard herself announce, "What I know how to be is married." Her arms in the mirror looked buff. She thought she could do fewer pull-ups and Teddy wouldn't notice.

After her workout shower, she dropped the rough, washed-thin gym towel and took a look at herself. First just a quick hip-and-ass glance as she walked to the lotion dispenser. Then facing herself straight on, Sabina worked the thick cream up her legs and stomach.

She thought she better look.

Because, again, why—it had to be asked—why all the actual, real-life attention, random smiles, sudden declarations? It seemed even colleagues had noticed, walking past her drafting table and saying things like "Nice dress, Sabina."

All in all, she looked like herself. Her legs were her same legs. Maybe a little bunchy around the knees. Her stomach—she could gather a handful of crepey skin—but that had been true since the kids were born. Her breasts—less up than down, nothing an underwire didn't lift. Sunspots, a fleshier neck, spider veins mapping the back of her legs. There was a thickening to her waist. But on the positive, thanks to Teddy—cut legs, no jiggly arms—she had muscles.

Was it some kind of age statistic? Some last hurrah of the body before its free fall into the progressive-lens cavern of late middle age? Was it a conspiracy, a biological imperative of the last non rancid, horny eggs, to have a spicy final fling?

Two turban-wrapped women came out of the steam room. They were laughing. "I bet you," one said, "not everyone would say that." The women exchanged quick looks and walked over to the mirror where Sabina stood.

"Excuse me, we need to ask you something," the other woman said.

They were all naked in front of the mirror. Whatever Sabina had noticed before now looked paler and droopier next to these younger bodies.

"We have a bottle of Jack Daniel's riding on this. Would you say you do or don't look back on your first boyfriends and feel embarrassed?" They were all talking to one another looking in the mirror.

"Wait, that is so not the question," the other woman said, and Sabina watched her knock into her friend. "The question is—if you could—no questions asked, current life not jeopardized—would you go for a night with all the old boyfriends again?"

Sabina said, "I met my husband when I was nineteen."

"Get out of here; that's awesome," one said, but they both looked as if Sabina had admitted that she was borderline retarded.

"We've been split up for two years," Sabina said, aware that she was standing naked, confessing to naked strangers. "And I've just started sleeping in the middle of the king-size bed."

One of the young woman put her hand on Sabina's shoulder. "We should probably buy you the Jack Daniel's."

The next Saturday, she didn't want to sit next to Tomaso at the dinner given for Antonio's sister, who was visiting from Barcelona. But it wouldn't have mattered if Sabina had wanted to, since Marley had made heart-shaped place cards. Sabina was seated between Antonio and a French cardiologist.

"We were so jealous to hear you had dinner with Tomaso,"

Antonio said.

"Of Tomaso or of me?" Sabina said.

When exactly she had become this flirty, cheeky woman, she didn't know. She hated that Tomaso had told them—even if he'd only boasted about his fabulous cooking. Couldn't she have dinner with a man? She wasn't breaking any law or vow. She was single. She hadn't ever been single before. She never used the word *single* before she was married, and even these last two years she hadn't once thought she was single. But now she was. And she could do anything she wanted. She could even make love with Antonio and Marley and Tomaso if she wanted.

Sabina turned to the French cardiologist and asked about a patent she'd overheard him speaking about before dinner. There was apparently another doctor in California who was working on a similar valve. It was a race, the cardiologist said, "and we are neck and neck."

It sounded, with his accent, that the doctor was saying, *we are naked neck.*

Sabina was trying to stay in the conversation, but now an image had stuck in her head. She felt certain Antonio had seen it too and was waiting patiently for her to turn back to him. It really was as if it had already happened: Her kneeling naked on the floor, kissing his naked wife. Him in a chair, watching. Him coming over to sit behind her, reaching around to fit his hand inside her.

"I am trying so hard," the cardiologist said. Sabina saw how exhausted the man looked, like he might drop his fork.

"Maybe you need to step away from the race and take a holiday." Sabina realized she didn't know what she was talking about. Everything tonight felt like a posture. Saying *holiday* instead of *vacation*. Pretending she was single when what she was was divorced. Having fantasies when she was a person who didn't have fantasies.

She wanted to go home, put on sweatpants, walk the dog, and make sure her daughter came in by curfew.

"It is not just a race. The work is important." The cardiologist, with his messy curls, strong nose, and intense gaze, looked more like a French actor playing a doctor than any doctor Sabina knew. He held his knife in place while his fork pushed into the slice of steak. "I have to finish what I must do. But now we are at a party, and I must suffer so many beautiful women at one table."

Then suddenly—well, not exactly suddenly, but as if the first vision had unleashed more, like going from frigid to torrentially orgasmic—Sabina was a person who had fantasies.

This one involved—this was so sorry-assed she couldn't believe it—the dude with the nose ring. She would have liked if it had been someone else—the French cardiologist would have been fabulous, even Tomaso—really, practically anyone else would have been good. But it was the dude with the nose ring who followed her into a dimly lit office stairwell and propped her against the steel banister, telling her to lean back and trust him. And did it even count as a fantasy if Sabina wondered, "Should I really trust a guy who pokes holes in his own face?"

But like it or not, it was an actual fantasy, since now it seemed the dude had a tongue piercing too, and while Sabina, in her normal-go-about-her-life-mind, thought tongue piercing was gross and sure to breed infection, she liked the way the ball bit of metal felt when she leaned back, braced perilously on the banister just outside her office, and he started working on her.

"Didn't we ever?" Sabina asked her ex. "Don't you think it's weird we didn't?"

"No, this is what's weird." He looked pleadingly at Sabina. The conversation about college finance planning had ended, and Sabina and her ex stayed at their red Formica kitchen table, the one they had bought in one of the kitchen supply shops on the Bowery, since renovated into a club with a Saigon-circa-1940s look.

"Then just pretend this is a professional sex survey and it's not me asking."

"But it is you. The kids are right in the other room. I'm not really comfortable talking about this."

"That's not question one," Sabina said. "'Are you comfortable talking about your desires' is way, way down the survey list."

It was hard at first to figure out who was crying on the phone. When Sabina realized it was Marley, she realized that what Marley was saying over and over was "I don't know what to do."

"What's going on?" Sabina had the phone crooked in her neck so she could keep chopping red peppers. She wished she had waited and let the answering machine pick up the call.

"You're one of the only people I can call," Marley said. Her voice sounded so young. "Antonio's away for the week and I've been with them all day and they're both so sick and now they have terrible coughs that sound like they're seals." It took Sabina a little bit to realize the call had nothing to do with Antonio. It was the twins.

"That's croup," Sabina explained. "My youngest had it for years. I'll be right over."

When Sabina got to the apartment, she brought Marley and the babies straight into the bathroom and turned the shower handle fully to hot.

"Strip down. It's going to get really steamy in here." Sabina wriggled out of her T-shirt without letting go of one of the babies.

Marley looked so frightened.

"We've got to get it hot. But it's going to be okay, Marley."

The women waited with babies in their arms while the bathroom filled with steam. They were sweating, their hair sticking against their faces and the babies' skin. Sabina passed off a baby to Marley. She stripped down out of her jeans, put up her hair, and then coiled Marley's long hair, using a toothbrush as a hairpin to hold it off Marley's damp neck. Then Sabina settled the baby back on her shoulder. Marley handed the second baby over so she could take off her leggings and shirt.

Sabina told Marley how, for a while, every time her son had a cold he became croupy. They would do it tonight just like Sabina had learned to do it. First twenty minutes in full steam. Which is what the two women did together, sitting in their wet bras and underpants till the twins' breathing regulated. Then Sabina guided Marley and the sleeping twins and they sat by an open window. The women were quiet. The air was cool and pleasant.

"Can I get you something?" Marley said. It was halfhearted; Sabina could see Marley was exhausted. She looked like a kid who'd been kept up too late babysitting.

"Why don't you sleep?" Sabina said. "They're good now for a while. I'll stay. If you want, I can stay the night."

"You'd do that? You'd stay with me?"

"I don't have a better offer," Sabina said. The two women laughed. Marley leaned back against Sabina. Sabina could feel Marley's skin was damp and goosefleshed too. Sabina pulled the toothbrush from Marley's hair and fingered through it to help loosen any knots. Marley's hair smelled of sweat and shampoo.

"Antonio won't be able to even imagine what this was like," Marley whispered, half-asleep. "That was scary."

"They grow out of this," Sabina said. "But you can't believe what comes next."

It was good then, that night, first by the window with the sounds of people outside enjoying the easy weather, and then when the women crawled into Marley and Antonio's bed, their skin cooled and dry and the children tucked between them.

STUFF

"Is this really the way you think I want to remember my mother?" he asked, shaking out the endless little bits of things stuck to the bottom of the pocketbook—unwrapped sticky sucking things, loose capsules, a split and dirty pill, receipts and then more receipts—for what? he couldn't tell—and did he need to see every piece of paper and see what the hell crazy products his mother bought at yet another rip-off store?

He dropped a metal hair clip on the bed. "This is quite a way for you to meet my mother."

The girlfriend looked up from where she was sitting close to him and said, "Do you not want me here? Tell me. Do you want to do this by yourself?"

"Just tell me if you want this," he snipped, pinching open the metal hair clip between his thumb and forefinger. "If you don't, I'll chuck it."

Actually, he wanted to chuck the whole thing out, toss all these lost days of being back in this clutter. Fuck the piles for Goodwill. Let alone her rooms of papers and her closets to sort through. He would throw the house out if he could. But here, now, first, was the shit in her pocketbook. Why exactly did a woman like her actually need so much plastic?

He sneered at the girlfriend, who was leaning in close to the mirror, pinning her bangs into a spit curl. He admired the planked stretch of the girlfriend's back, and her serious face in his mother's mirror, and he thought he'd better not start thinking about how damn good she looked in his mother's room. He needed to just get to it. Might as well get on the phone—wasn't that how it was done?—call and say his mother wouldn't be needing these credit cards, and he would have to listen while women with every kind of cheerful accent said, "You're the son? Oh, I'm so sorry."

He'd heard nothing but sorry women on phones for days and nights. Last night, just as he'd drifted off, an old neighbor called all teary, asking how could it all happen so quickly after such a life as the life she'd seen. "So tell me," he'd accused, his eyes sharpening in the dark room. "What did she see?"

The neighbor's voice stiffened. "This and that. You know her. Nothing you need to think about."

If he was lucky enough to get a woman on the phone.

Women could do things for him, he knew. No, no, he needn't start sending proof of anything. They would send him the last statement, make a note, and that would take care of everything. "My God," the women would say, "this is the last thing a son should have to deal with." They understood. They could hear it in his voice what kind of son he was and they wanted to help out—even in such little ways as they had to offer.

The girlfriend wanted to do things too. So was it so wrong the way he'd let her take care when all his mother's friends came back to the house? He stood in the doorway then, watching her move, lithe among his mother's arthritic friends. The girlfriend, carrying platters of sliced meats into the dining room, stopped to lean close to him, whispering, "I'll talk to them. I'll take care of it. You go rest."

"This one's a keeper and such a looker," the women called to him, loudly, with chewed bits of pumpernickel in the corners of their mouths. "Did she meet your mother?" He imagined how he would have suffered, moody and silent, watching her make eager talk with his mother. And the girlfriend—what could she have eaten of his mother's burnt foods, roasts and goulash, everything thick and gelled with gravy? This girlfriend, he loved the way she ate, seaweeds and long radishes that she steamed for her dinner. He even loved watching the way food rested on her fork as if the fork was a sort of prayer. But seeing her in the living room, talking with the old women, her hands steadying the wobbly saucers of his mother's glued china, he thought she actually looked a little like them. A skinny new-world version. A thickness lurking about her nose. Even her boyish hips looked on the verge of swelling large.

The girlfriend had found him later, fitting herself against him on his boy-size bed.

"Hey, you never even fell asleep. I finally got the last of them out of here," she whispered, reaching around to stroke him. She cupped him in her hands. "Would this make you feel a little better?"

All the nights he'd spent conjuring girl hands in this room!

He hunched closer to the wall, as if refusing her were the best comfort he could manage.

But now the girlfriend, all pretty and leggy in only his buttoned shirt, was at the mirror, fingering pots of creams for every minute of day and night and holding one after another lipstick up to her lips. His mother's lipsticks. His mother's smeared mirror. How many times had he come into the room and found his mother staring at herself, or calling him over to help her with the high place on her zipper where her hands couldn't get to? He couldn't count how many times he'd zipped, but he could count the one, maybe two times he had bothered to say, hooking the clasp into the eye, "You're looking nice, Mom." And seeing himself now in the mirror, holding his mother's dumped-out pocketbook, he was ashamed at all her stuff and ashamed at all the one-word answers he ever gave her.

"Do you want to do the drawers?" the girlfriend asked, twisting an orange lipstick into its silver holder.

"Do you think I do?" he sneered, looking down at the sunken shape of the emptied pocketbook.

"I don't have to be here, if you don't want," the girlfriend said. "It's fine. I can head back."

He remembered the sound of this house, days he'd rush home from school to have—what?—maybe an hour at the most alone. In his room, or playing records in the living room, or coming in and searching through his parents' bureau drawers for something new he'd never found. He'd reach in, scrounging around, unpairing socks, mad there wasn't any secret. There was always ordinary stuff: socks and coins. Even his mother's silky things felt plain. Those years, he'd worn his mother's lipstick more than once and liked it mostly for the waxy taste when he licked it off.

"I guess we better do it," he said, forcing his eyes back up to see her in the mirror, and seeing himself there, pale, unwashed, he saw what the girlfriend could not recognize in him—his mother's long face, her slack and heavy jaw. He tried to make his face shorter. His girlfriend, in his button-down shirt, looked like something that might blow away, looked like all the silky things he had wanted to find in his parents' drawers.

"But first let's take a break." He fell back on the pile he'd dumped out from the pocketbook. Then, waving his hands like a drowning man, he said, "If you come lie on top of me and do every dirty thing you can think of, I'll let you take all the lipsticks you want."

"They said things," the girlfriend said. She was relaxed on top of him, her knuckles working at pressure points in his face.

"Who," he said.

"Your mother's ladies," she said.

"Whoa. Must have been fascinating," he said.

"Actually, it was. But I shouldn't say anything," she said.

"What? Say what?"

"Nothing, just stuff women say, you know."

"I don't know. Do I look like I know?" he said.

"Nothing. I mean, nothing that's really going to change anything," she said, pressing her fingers tightly against his temples.

"My father used to sleep on this side." He rolled out from under her. "He said it was the only way he'd ever sleep because she was up and down half the night."

"Why?" asked the girlfriend. "Why was she up?"

He looked at her smooth legs, lifted and scissoring the air. She looked like something that had never woken in the wrong hours of night, something that could fall asleep in any corner and stay dreamless and asleep until morning.

What did she think she was trying to do, relaxing him?

"I guess she couldn't sleep. But for all I know, maybe she wanted to do more housework." He wanted to roll right the fuck over, pull his pants on, and get back to work. What did he think he was doing, losing most of the morning with the girlfriend doing some woolo-woolo thing above him? It was time to stop doodling around and call the customer-service women, or at least just get the girlfriend up and off his parents' bed. Though really, what was the big deal? It was just a bed in a fucking room. Hadn't his mother even offered, more than once, to give up her room for him and a lady friend if he came out for a visit? That was how his mother said it—*lady friend*—so that he was always teasing into the phone, "I don't even know a single *lady*, Mother."

"Was she always unhappy or something back then?" the girl-friend asked, her tan legs still scissoring. She pointed and flexed her painted red toes. She was always in motion, the girlfriend, always in a constant flush of aerobic activity. She was elastic; it seemed there wasn't any way he couldn't bend her legs. She was skinny and skinny-chested, too, and he remembered that when he'd thought about it, he'd thought his father must have fallen for his mother's large breasts.

"What's this?" the girlfriend said, pulling up in some yoga sit-up position, twisting her torso impossibly to reach around her back. "Man, I'm getting stabbed by your mother's keys."

"Back when?" he said. He slid open the bedroom closet. What did his mother suddenly need pantsuits for? And not just one, but maybe five, and in fancy newfangled fabrics. Where could she have been going in all these clothes? There were straw beach baskets and silly hats with visors. And long batik dresses. Sarongs. They were from the trips she'd told him about, her cruises to Mexico and Finland.

"I really needed that getaway," his mother, just back from the Greek islands, had announced over the phone. "And, okay, I admit it, I adore vacationing."

"Vacationing?" he'd asked, surfing back and forth between movies.

"It's such great, great fun," his mother had said about the ships. Fun? When had his mother first started talking about *fun*? When had she begun using words like *adore*? And why this going on ships when he could barely remember her ever wanting to leave the house? He was used to seeing his mother all day in housecoats, and here, smushed between the new stretchy things, were one or two that he remembered, loose floral affairs with buttons missing, so he could not help but see too much flesh.

Holding up shriveled pantyhose, the girlfriend said, "Look, you can't give this kind of thing away. I'm going to throw these out."

"It's not fair you knowing anything I don't know. Does it seem right to you?" he said.

"Didn't she ever talk to you? What did your mom tell you when she called every week?"

He tried to pull back anything his mother had said to him when she called. She was always too much with the talking, as his father used to say. "You are talking me to death," his father had shouted, and sometimes he'd say it, too, like a long-distance family joke: "Okay, I've gotta hang up. You've talked me to death."

"I don't know. She said things," he said, holding up a silk wrap skirt. After his mother came back from her California trip, she'd called to say she was home.

"How was California?" he'd managed to ask her.

"Too much on the bus," she'd said. "I'm too old for all that sitting." Now he imagined her in bright skirts up on ship decks, shopping in duty-free ports. Maybe there was line dancing. Casino nights.

"What do I want from these same old faces?" she'd said when he asked why she went on the trips alone. "I want to meet people."

"These are cool," the girlfriend said, fitting her fingers inside a pair of pink suede gloves and blowing a flurry of kisses. "I definitely want these." But the gloves looked like something the girlfriend already must have owned, something she would show up wearing in the parts of town where she was always arranging dinner parties. All he remembered was his mother in his father's winter gloves and his father shouting, "Go get your own gloves!"

"You're really not going to say anything?" he said.

"You're making a big deal of nothing. Look, it's nothing to get nuts about. Even your mother gets to have some privacy," the girlfriend said.

"You don't know my fucking mother," he said, thinking of the afternoons he'd come into a darkened house and found her still in bed. "You caught me," his mother had said to him.

"You're right." The girlfriend pulled off the narrow suede gloves and laid them palm-to-palm on the bureau top. "I'm getting out of here for a little while.

"Great." he said. "Fine. Leave if you want."

"I'm just going out to get more garbage bags to help you with all this stuff."

He sat cross-legged on his parents' bed, one of the worn floral housecoats tented over his head. He had not been in the house alone since he'd come back. Instead there were always the concerned questions of his girlfriend. A few grunting widowers. But, mostly, the house rattled with the ladies bunched on the living room sofa. "That gal, she could tell a joke," he'd heard one say. "Remember her line about marriage and a spare husband?" The stray men had looked up and laughed right along with the ladies.

Hadn't he sat on the stoop with his mother and these same ladies?

He could think of her non-stop yakking, but could he remember his mother ever telling anything like a joke?

Here, finally in the quiet, he wondered, where had he been? There had been afternoons heaped on years that he couldn't get out of being right there in her range, close enough for his mother to yank his collar down, lick her finger to smudge dirt off his cheek. He heard her even when he was slamming a ball against the garage wall, or, later, sneaking inside for the quick minutes it took to jerk off. Even then, angled against the green bathroom tiles, he could hear his mother outside the window and thought he'd never get far enough away from all her talk.

But it was obvious to him now that he'd missed it all. Seen nothing. Or just wrong things. Tented under her cotton housecoat, on his parents' bed, nobody could say he didn't know that smell. He'd found the mother he could recognize on the housedress, buried among all the new things. He could breathe her right in. He was surrounded by his mother.

His parents' room actually looked pretty, scrimmed through the orange dahlia dress print. He piled together the wallet and keys and scraps from her purse. He would look at everything, even the chipped pills, the lint and hair clumps, the dirty coins. He would slow down. There was an agenda book that velcroed shut. It might take the rest of the day, but he'd go through it carefully.

He opened the agenda book; papers and cards jabbed out. There were ads—toasters and raincoats on final sale at the department store. In the last section, an address book had names. Maybe he should call, one by one, all the names he didn't recognize. Some lived in different states. But what was he going to hear? That some lady in Seattle sat a bridge fourth on the Winter Blues Cruise? Or listen while some guy young enough to be his brother piped up, "Oh, you're her son? She was in our folk-dancing group. Quite the polka girl. A mom like that. You're lucky." Or, worse, he'd hear quiet on the other end and then, "You're sure? You found my name in her address book? I'm racking my brain. But I'm pretty sure, really. I'm sorry. I don't think I know her."

He shook the agenda book and a wad of envelopes fell from pages. He slipped off the rubber band. There was a bill from the electric company, a bill from the podiatrist, a late notice from the phone company and a handwritten letter obviously refolded and reread more than once.

He read as far as the salutation—*Dear Full-Figured Lady*—and knew this was no saved newsy letter from one of her ladies wintering down on a boardwalk. He read further and knew the man was not old, not a lonely widow, but a young man, with, as he put it, *a taste for the mature woman who knows what life is all about.* This discerning man thought she sounded perfect. *Could they meet for dinner? Theater?* He said he could already picture them window-shopping at night along the avenues. Together they didn't have to be lonely. She should know, he really needed her to know, that while this wasn't the first response he had ever written, this was the one he felt would be the true one, the genuine article. *Crazy!* he wrote. *But isn't following your heart a little crazy?*

Signed, *Hopefully yours, Brian.*

It was dated two years earlier. Two years his mother carried the letter around in her pocketbook. Transferred it seasonally from leather bag to straw bag. From the looks of the paper creases, the folding tears, he didn't want to know how many times she'd read the letter. He took his mother's dress off his head and shut his eyes. He could bet on his own fucking life that his mother never called this Brian. Or any Brian. He knew it like he knew he was his mother's son.

"Is this garbage or donation?" The girlfriend's voice was suddenly close by, careful, adjusted.

"What?" he asked, his eyes still shut.

"Touristy stuff. Castanets. You know, stuff you buy because you're there."

"Where? Where did she go?" he asked, opening his eyes. The girlfriend was wearing an embroidered fez. She held up a tied, full garbage bag. The room was a wreck of his mother's stuff.

The girlfriend crawled onto his mother's bed beside him. She was still holding the garbage bag. "It would easier if you could tell what you need."

"I need to know what she was doing?" he asked.

The girlfriend placed a hand flat on his forehead. "She was just living. That's all, baby," she said. She pressed her palm against his skull. "It's nice. Your mom was living it up."

He leaned against the filled-up garbage bag. There was something hard that poked back at him. Alone, without him or his father, she'd practically busted the seams of this house. His mother's closet, his dad's closet, even the closet in his old room was jammed to the top shelves. He felt his girlfriend, her steady hand, the easy stretch of her as she curled around him. Let her think he'd had a mother who was Living It Up. He would meet this girl in any part of their city at any hour. Maybe he'd look up at a corner and see her across the street, waving her bright, gloved fingers. He'd take a deep breath. He'd cross over to where she smiled and waved. He'd say yes when she asked if his day had been good. Yes, he'd say to whatever she asked. Maybe he'd be lucky enough to let his breath be taken away.

THE THIRD CYCLE

WHAT IT ALL MEANS NOW, HERE, AT THIS TABLE UNDER THE GREEN awning, is that neither woman can drink the wine that the impossibly boyish waiter offers, cheering, "Go on, ladies, go wild! One glass! It's spring."

What it also means is that both women have sworn not to mention the B word.

But that word keeps coming up and passing by on the street in prams, pushed by unachievably young women barely out of diapers themselves, or by women just the right age, effortless, and a bit established in their careers, or that word rolls past pushed by bulky women hired to walk imported prams. And all these women look smug, all of them look so fucking smug, the two women agree, like they never had a goddamn complication with anything in their goddamn perfect lives.

"I could use being someone else today," says one of the women.

"You? Call me Polly and I've got to be happier than who I am," the other woman says, squeezing at her arm.

"Polly? Right. That's perfect. You're Perky Polly and I'll be a Susie," says the new Susie.

"Just water?" repeats the waiter. "Are you sure?"

"Yes, yes," Polly and Susie say, practically in unison, suddenly disappointed, not for themselves—though it would be wonderful, just great, to have a midday glass of wine on the first warm, eating-outside day of the year, it being, of course, exactly what the women want, and never more than right now when God knows they could use a little old-fashioned, slightly drunk feeling—but disappointed for the waiter, that handsome candy of a boy. They are especially disappointed that in his eagerness to give them pleasure, they've denied him the opportunity to provide a good time, and it makes the two women so sorry, as sorry as if he were their clumsy, disappointed first lover.

They are really trying to have a good time, acting a little tipsy even, angling recklessly toward the sun, though both women know that especially now they are sensitive—but what the fuck, they agree, if they have no apparent heirs, they might as well look fabulous and die young.

They've made promises.

They've promised not to compare treatments or new measures or the terrible percentages, those absolutely unimaginable shrinking percentages, the tiny tiny tiny positive number they've had to imagine squeezing their bloated selves into, knowing the impossible odds of either, let alone both, women fitting in. And what exactly are those percentages? They can't either of them remember, one-quarter or half a percent? Or is that with no treatments?

No, this is off-limits, that talk.

And forget about oranges, though how can they forget?—Polly and Susie, they trade orange stories.

"I think I'm feeling good, Susie, really," says Polly.

"Really?" says Susie. "Then let's swap names in a few minutes."

~

How can they not talk oranges?

Polly saying it hadn't been too encouraging at all practicing on the orange, seeing the way she had to poke and jab at it, like the peel was some kind of elephant hide, poking and probing till she had stabbed an actual hole in the fucking piece of fruit before she got the needle in. "Forget it," she says. When it was time for her own pebbled skin, she was up and at the clinic, where there was someone who got paid to poke a bunch of scaredy-cats.

"You should have called me," boasts Susie, happy to have something to boast about. "I was a goddamn killer with that needle. I'd have been happy to do you."

But enough!

Enough needles!

Enough drugs! No drugs.

They swear they won't talk about drugs. The D word. "Unless," says Susie, "unless we're talking about some bliss we can get off a simple fucking dealer."

But here, loose-hipped and friendly, is the waiter again, saying, "There are some awesome specials you ladies might just like." They don't like that, *ladies,* the way he says *ladies,* like they are so far away from him, ladies, in another world, untouchable, quaint creatures.

Here is the waiter saying, "What about some awesome salsas and rocking tapenades?" And, of course, of course, there's always the obligatory ladies' grilled chicken.

"So what'll it be?" asks the waiter, bouncing in his own wake.

"We just want fresh, viable eggs," says Polly.

"Eggs! Eggs! More eggs!" they shriek, "Lots and lots of them!" and the both of them are laughing now, unladylike, practically snorting water right at the waiter. They squeal cautions at him like "Just tell the cook not to scramble them" and "Use a bowl and not a petri dish," and the waiter laughs along, though God knows at what, the two women say after he scampers off, and they double over, laughing, losing it all again when Susie catches her breath to squeal, "At the fucking sorry barnyard sight of us, my dear."

Okay, no D words.

But here is a Point of Information. And information is, after all, what the women hope will help. Like tube information. Tube statistics. Like statistics that show that the tube is a better place, maybe the best place for any formal introductions.

One woman knows a woman who knows a woman who went to a clinic where they made the women eat red dirt.

And who is to say meditation, visualization, even a little chanting might not help?

"Let's talk about fucking," says Susie in a quiet, serious voice.

"Oh, that's not part of any procedure," says Polly.

"No, I mean the old kind. Just a fuck kind of fuck," Susie says a little too seriously. "Please, I need us to talk about that."

But Polly looks sad and says, "I'm tired all the time from just thinking."

Then the B word comes in closer, wheels up to the next table in a hooded blue pram, and a woman wearing matching blue sits and locks her leg around the pram like it might wheel away of its own accord.

It occurs silently to both of them that the Blue Woman has done certain things right in her life that both of these women have not done right.

It occurs silently to both of them that the Blue Woman's presence is an insult.

It occurs to both of them that a woman might go out shopping for a pram and dress it up, outfit it with sweet checkered bumpers and cotton blankets, even a cloth diaper draped for swabbing up spittle, that a woman might take that pram out to a restaurant on a spring day, order a lemon iced tea and sit for hours, cooing and fussing into a perfect, empty pram.

But this Blue Woman reaches in and lifts out an actual blue-capped baby, singing, "Here we are. Here we are. Here we are."

The waiter is back, all chummy and chipper, dipping this way with a fruit platter and leaning across the table with a flourish, setting the lunch chicken down.

"Your eggs," he says with a wink.

The women watch him walk off. He stands with a group of other waiters. They hear him, still chirping, leaning in close to a young waitress, who laughs and pokes his side with a fork.

"There was a time I'd have fucked that waiter before he was done with this shift," says Susie.

"Did you?" says Polly, as if suddenly realizing she has known nothing of her friend's life.

"Trust me, worse."

"So tell me," says Polly, but she looks down at her chicken, picking at the striped grilled flesh.

"Well, God, once I made a man—" Susie begins, but Polly waves her hands and says, "No. No B word. No D word. No M or F word."

"What's left?"

"Lunch."

"Oh," says Susie, wiping a bread crust around and around her plate, "that's too easy. I'm hungry all the time."

The Blue Woman at the next table eats and talks to the pram. "Just sleep now, please," she says, her leg locked around the pram, jiggling the wheels, so the blue hood bounces. "That's my sweetie," says the Blue Woman, "that's a good baby letting me eat my lunch."

"May I ask a question?" Susie asks, after the waiter takes away the plates.

"That really depends," answers Polly.

"Can I tempt you?" asks the waiter, back now with something whipped.

～

"I don't feel very Pollyish anymore," says Polly.

"Well if you think of the alternative, you might try a little harder," Susie says, spooning up a heap of the whipped thing.

No B word, but here is the Blue Woman trying to fit the red-faced B on her breast and unsweetly saying, "You just couldn't let me have my lunch first, could you?"

"I'll hold her," bursts Polly, suddenly reaching out beyond her table and touching the Blue Woman's arm. "Call me Polly."

"No," says the Blue Woman, drawing back in surprise. "I mean, I'm sorry if we're disturbing your lunch or something."

"Hardly," says Polly. "I know how it can be."

"That's really very nice of you," says the Blue Woman. The baby is bleating, a frantic, gulpy bleat of a cry.

"I could help," says Polly and holds out her hands in a most open manner.

The Blue Woman is reluctant—and why shouldn't she be? A stranger? And she is embarrassed. Can't calm her own child? Can't get her own baby to shut up? "But really, it's too much. I shouldn't," she says, handing the bundle of baby over.

"It's perfectly fine." Polly takes the baby, who is arching this and that way, a wriggle of complaint. "I'm used to this."

Polly watches the Blue Woman begin to eat.

Susie watches Polly holding the baby up high on her shoulder, bouncing it, bouncing it too hard, Susie thinks, and the baby's neck—should it be let to wobble like that? Susie reaches out her hand to guard the neck, and she touches the blue bonnet, which is scratchier than she thinks is right for a baby's bonnet. Polly yanks the baby in closer.

The Blue Woman is eating, making almost grunting sounds.

"Excuse me," says the Blue Woman. "You'll think I'm exaggerating, but this is the first meal that's had any taste since I had this baby. How can I thank you?"

The baby scooches up on Polly's shoulder. Polly twists her head toward the little baby legs, her mouth munching up a wriggling leg. "Yummy, yummy, yummy," she says kissing the leg. Susie reaches to take the baby away from Polly, which she does with a firm hand, though the baby's head flops before she can curl around it, resting it down in her lap. The baby is plump, with full, plum cheeks. "Is this delicious or what?" Susie says, leaning over the baby, making smoochy nibble kisses.

"I could eat this one up," says Susie. "I could just eat her right up." And it looks to Polly like Susie might eat the baby right up, the way she opens her mouth over the chubby fingers.

"I mean it, food has never tasted so good," says the Blue Woman. "Can I buy you another dessert or something?"

"We'll just keep it," Susie declares, and Polly smiles.

"Yes," says Polly, "that seems like a fair trade."

The Blue Lady is eating with her face practically right down in her plate. She doesn't even look up when she asks, "How many do you have? You're both so easy at it. Yours are out of the house?"

"None in the house," says Polly, smiling at Susie. "But we're ready, just really ready to get more."

"That's brave," laughs the Blue Woman, her mouth full of food. "I can't even manage one."

"It works out, trust me," says Polly, reaching across to bow the baby's loose bonnet strings.

"God, I hope so." The Blue Woman puts her fork down on her plate. "I'll take over now. I better before you think I'm a total misfit."

"No," snaps Susie, pulling the baby in tight against her chest.

Polly smiles at Susie.

"No really, it's fine, I'm done with my lunch," says the Blue Woman, folding her napkin.

Polly and Susie clutch in. They narrow together so close that the baby disappears between them.

"Thank you so much for the help but the baby needs to eat a bit," says the Blue Woman. She opens her hands toward the women.

"We'll feed it," Polly says through her full smile.

"Not a problem," says Susie, "really."

"But I need my baby now," says the Blue Woman, her hands pushed down in Susie's lap, wrestling the bonneted thing free.

"What kind of mother pulls her own child like that?" squeals Polly.

And Susie stands, shouting over and over, something the waiter thinks is "No, I need it!" so that he jumps from where he's been clowning around, braiding his hair together with two waitresses', to go see what exactly this ranting nut of a customer needs.

He skids up to the table, pleading, "Ladies, I beg of you, is there a problem somewhere?"

But now it is the Blue Woman's turn.

Now she is efficient, unbuttoning her blouse, but doing so very slowly, so the two women and the waiter all stop, riveted as the blue shirt yields under her fingers, then the white unhooked stretch of brassiere, then the creamy swell of skin—teased and insisted forth.

But a sudden wind, so sudden—this is, after all, just the beginning of spring—gusts under the green awning so it presses up in a furious, swollen bulge. Susie's skirt whooshes up in a girlish petal. Polly shelters glasses from knocking over. The waitresses shimmy close to one another. Maybe this weather should be enough of a problem to stop all foolishness. An antic wind to disrupt the first spring out-of-doors lunch.

No, it must be even more extreme.

Then torrents of rising water, plagues of frogs interrupting traffic, vermin wreaking havoc on sidewalk fruit vendors.

Of course, slaying of the firstborn has been, if not mentioned, already considered.

But nothing now can stop the Blue Woman. She surprises herself, quite amazed, as though she were some other woman entirely. In this other life, out pops a full breast, all the way into a fuller view than is needed to lift its veined weight, to urge the little rooting mouth to fix on the wide, dark nipple.

In this life, the baby latches on too tightly and the Blue Woman cringes and pulls herself free. A spray of milk spits against the baby's stunned face. She smiles greedily at the two women when the baby closes back onto her breast.

"Hey, let me in," says the waiter, rushing to knit himself in with the waitresses. And out there, on the crowded lunchtime street, at least one of the women passing is in the third cycle. One remembers a dream with crows. One spots. One ferns. One argues with her long-dead mother about beige shoes. One dilates. Some release multiple buds. One feels a kick. Some bleed. One flashes. One is not ready. Many have just finished. Ready or not, it is onward and onward to desk and laboratory and home and conference call and bank and shop. Not one, but all, waits to see if she can.

THE NORTH TRAIN

MADAME S. DID NOT WANT TO GET ON THE TRAIN. IT DID NOT MATTER that every Thursday for the last two years she had boarded the north-bound train, riding to the town where her old pupil ran a ballet school. It did not matter that every Thursday for those two years she had never wanted to get on the train. She had been contracted by her pupil as a *master teacher*, but a master teacher of what?—a school of ballet in the basement of a town church? All she ever saw on her Thursdays in the low-ceilinged church basement were girls who heard no music and girls who had the souls—not to mention the feet—of rhinos. This is what Madame S. was asked to suffer.

She could show them feet. Even with her low-heeled tie shoes, Madame S. could show the girls how feet should look.

"Hello, Madame S.," the girls chimed each Thursday afternoon when she stepped into the basement room. The girls lined up at the barre, their hair bunned and wrapped in nets, their legs layered in loosely knit and frayed leg-warmers—outfits pitifully copied from magazine photos of real dancers in rehearsal. The girls hung on the barre, practicing frappé and ronde de jambe.

Once Madame S. had hissed into a girl's ear, "You think you can learn one thing ballet when you can't even pronounce my simple Russian name?" She made the girl hold an arabesque until she could properly pronounce the crush of consonants in Madame S.'s surname. For the rest of the class, the girl's shoulders shook, as she tried to hold back her crying. Later, after dinner at the director's home, her old pupil had said, "Svetlana, it's easier, please, Madame S. This isn't Moscow. They'll botch your name."

This was not Moscow! What a thing even to say. What could Madame S. expect? Hadn't the director herself only ever been a second-rate dancer? The very idea that her pupil, Adrienne, called herself *Director of Ballet* Madame S. found a joke. Sickled feet, no instep, at best a character dancer on the weekend pas de deux circuit. Maybe once, one season, one spot in the corps de ballet of Sadler's Wells. The kind of young woman who, with luck, might parlay a middling career into marriage with a young man who found ballet dancers exotic. And then to live in a nice house with dinners served on silver-plated trays—Madame S. could see her old pupil had herself a little luck. A nice house in this nice town was proof a dance career had come to something after all.

Madame S. stood on the train platform and thought, No more on the train.

A conductor stopped next to her. "Metro North to North White Plains," he said quietly.

"I don't want to get on," whispered Madame S.

"There's a problem?" the conductor asked, touching the sleeve of her black wool coat. "Did something happen?"

Madame S. looked at the conductor. His head was too big. His hat was off-kilter, perched on the top of his head. He looked a little like a black Igor Paravich, a young man she had known in Moscow. Igor Paravich, even with his oversized head, had been a lovely turner—five, six pirouettes were nothing for Igor.

"Did something happen?" the black Igor Paravich asked again.

"Will you walk me to a seat?" she asked, lifting her arm.

The conductor looked around as if he might be breaking a rule. He took her small overnight case in one hand. With his other, he took hold of her by the sleeve.

"This is your train, right? The train is leaving soon." He led her into the car and to an empty seat. "Will this be all right for you?" he asked, placing her overnight case right next to her. He started to walk off, then stopped. "Miss, you stay there. I'll be back for your ticket."

Madame S. watched the black Igor walk off with his big, tilted head ready to pull him, hat and all, to the ground.

What a funny, lovely thought! That young man, silly Igor—she had not thought of him in maybe forty years. She had been crazy for Igor Paravich, following him day after day as he paraded around the studio hallways. She had practically corralled him into her bed, only to find that he kept knocking into her; he was more elbow than anything else in her bed. For all his triple pirouettes, he was a young man without rhythm in love.

And now to find him in America, a conductor and a black man at that!

Whatever her old pupil, the director, said, the girls in the ballet school were not nearly as afraid of Madame S. as she thought they should be. They talked among themselves while she showed them steps for the adagio. Or they called out, "Madame S., what comes after the port de bras?" In Russia, she'd never called out. Who would have thought of asking questions? Why, she had barely been able to look any of her instructors in the eye. Not even that first pig farmer of a teacher she had in her village. Or later, when she'd moved to Moscow, when she'd been noticed and pegged as next in line for the company, not even then, passing the director of ballet in the hallway, could she look up as she knew she should, with a vibrant and ready, "Good day, Sir." No, she could barely muster an audible anything.

Still, she'd been noticed by the director and she knew it, and at night in her tiny room in the boarding house, she'd hold the small mirror so she could see her body in patches, and piece by piece, she'd admire what she could see. Before bed, she'd take each foot in her hands. Pressing with all her strength on her insteps, she'd admire the way her feet bent almost like claws.

This Thursday, as on every Thursday, it was women who boarded the train. Not one of the women Madame S. watched—not the cream-colored woman with her tied-up shopping bags, not the cinnamon-colored woman with her country straw hat, not the woman with the tucked-down face that, to Madame S., looked gray—not one of these women Madame S. watched board the train and slip into a seat looked as if she were happy stepping on the train.

As far as Madame S. could see, the whole train was full of women not pleased to be going north.

Then Madame S. heard boys. They jammed into the train. There were three of them, gangly white boys, limbs loose-fitting and seeming to jut and bend at impossible angles. Their bodies looked modern. They swung into seats across the aisle from Madame S., each claiming a whole seat. They stretched out their legs; large sneakers dangled off into the aisle. Everything about the boys was loud, their slick jackets, their talk—and the words themselves were loud words, words Madame S. recognized from her neighborhood, worn proudly, like the boys' sloppy clothes.

"That's too fucked up," one of the boys shouted, slapping the top of the head of the boy seated in front of him. "I'm going to fuck you up, my man." The other boy whipped around, popped over the seat, saying, "What the fuck you got to fuck with me for?"

She heard a woman somewhere in the car say, "Please!"

"Oh, fuck off," one boy shouted, and all the boys laughed, then snickered to a quiet and slumped so low in their seats Madame S. could only see them by their bright, floppy sneakers. She was glad to have them in the car. She watched their large feet flexing and beating out constant rhythms and thought she'd have more luck with these loud, rude boys than with the girls she was going up to teach.

Madame S. reached into her handbag. She took out the piece of fruit she had brought for the ride. She did not like to eat on the train, but the lunch she had eaten in her apartment was not enough to hold her through the afternoon. It would be worse to hurriedly try and eat the apple between the children's class and the advanced girls' class. She had washed the apple before leaving her apartment and wrapped it in a cloth towel. But still, the apple looked funny under the fluorescent train lights, and Madame S. polished it against her thinned lambswool sweater. She held it in her lap.

The lights on the train flickered off and then back on. The train jerked, then started slowly out of the station tunnel. Madame S. closed her eyes so she did not have to watch the train break into sharp, flickering light as it picked up speed on the outdoor northbound tracks.

When she opened her eyes, it looked like a better place. Not a Moscow, but maybe a Saint Petersburg. Or a Hamburg. She had been to Hamburg, and Vienna too. And why hadn't it occurred to her before this day that this section of the trip looked a little like the forests and hamlets outside of Vienna? She had been on fire when she was in Vienna. It did not matter if she did one hundred fouettés or stood and simply pointed her foot—she had been on fire.

And after the performance there had been a man, a count or baron, with hideous floppy flowers and devotions. She laughed at his formalities, his pleading that she must wear her plumage and agree to a holiday at his estate by the sea. But she left Vienna before he returned with his driver. Madame S. had been happy riding the train out of Vienna with her crate of tutus aboard, her headpieces—the white Giselle headband, the Firebird tiara with long red and black feathers the seamstress had acquired at some cost from a dealer in exotic birds. She was leaving Vienna for Marseilles with the first violinist, a fast and thrashy man who, it turned out, liked her to walk up and down on his back while he begged for extreme punishments before he could finally settle into sleep.

Madame S. looked out the window of the train. They had left the wooded area and entered degraded, broken streets where the buildings were low and some close to the tracks were boarded up. They passed a tenement with the windows painted black. This was not Vienna or Marseilles. What had she been thinking? At least in the town where the school was, Madame S. was driven past large houses, houses large enough that a small baron might take up residence there.

The director's house was a modern, split-level house with clean Formica surfaces. Madame S. was given the youngest daughter's room to sleep in every Thursday night. The girl collected skeletons of fish-like creatures and rocks with plants embedded in them. The girl said they were fossils, and spoke of how and when they'd lived as if she'd been alive that long ago. She handed Madame S. a piece of stone that looked like a cockroach and said it was Paleozoic, more than 250 million years old. The first night, Madame S. thought she'd never get to sleep with all the shelves of strange, ancient things in the girl's room. But now, every Thursday night, Madame S. barely had time to rub cream on her feet before she was asleep.

The conductor was back in the car, stalling in the aisles. "Tickets," he called in the same good voice he had used with her on the platform. What had she seen before? He looked nothing like Igor Paravich—black or anywise. Igor was wiry and this man was all bulk, a wide body and head. He moved thickly, stopping to punch tickets.

"Tickets, please," he said.

"Tickets," he said, pausing with his hand punch beside each seat.

He came to the first of the boys. "Why don't you just sit up nice and take those off the seats." The boy said nothing, and Madame S. watched his large feet brightly beating out some rhythm. "I said, get yourself up, please."

Madame S. watched the conductor reach down and grab the top of the boy's shirt.

"Don't let me catch you with your feet up again," the conductor said, but as soon as the conductor roughly let go of the boy's shirt and pressed his way through the aisles, nodding at Madame S. as he punched her ticket and continued out of the car, the boy had already slipped down and stretched out his legs, scraping his sneakers against the seat until they stuck into the aisle, his sneakers twitching, jumping in a way that looked very much like a well-schooled changement de pieds.

Madame S. took a bite of her apple. Then another, so that her mouth was a little uncomfortably full. "Go fuck off, Igor," she whispered, hoping the boy might turn around so she could smile a messy, pulpy smile, and let him know that she was on his side.

Madame S. looked out from the railway overpass, expecting to see her pupil, the school director, waiting as she did each week in the station turnaround, leaning against her car, ready to take Madame S.'s overnight case, opening the car door with a bow, saying, "You're here, Svetlana! How wonderful that you're here," as if Madame S. came on the train out of Moscow to a dacha for a little country vacation!

But the car was not there. Madame S. stood still on the overpass and looked toward the spot where the car should be waiting, as if she'd somehow missed seeing it. She could feel a tiny vibration in the cement overpass, as though her train had already pulled out of the station. Madame S. remembered that one time, in winter, her pupil had moved the car in among the parked cars and come running with big frozen breaths back to the car, waving and shouting, "I bought coffee. Don't try coming here, you'll slip and break your neck. I'll pull around." But looking over to the parked cars, Madame S. didn't see her pupil waving and realized she didn't recall the color of the car she'd been driven every Thursday. It wasn't red. Or white. But what color was it? Dark, she thought, blue, maybe. Or gray. Something metallic. Maybe silver?

It was probably as simple this time as that time in winter, Adrienne having ducked into a store for a coffee. Or she was late. She'd never been late, but it could happen. Really, anything could happen to delay her, even though she'd never been delayed before. Soon, the old pupil would pull in to the turnaround, tooting her horn, flustered, apologetic. They might even be late for class.

Madame S. should go and wait by the turnaround. Others waited. Two dark ladies. A girl with a backpack. But Madame S. could also stay here, on the overpass, above the empty track, where she had a bigger view and could probably spot her pupil pulling into the station and get down to the turnaround by the time the car pulled up. Madame S. was sure that even if she didn't remember the color, she'd know the car as soon as she saw it.

She had never before lingered on the overpass. From here, things looked different. Or actually were different. Had she gotten off at the wrong stop? A stop shy? What then? She looked for a reassuring marker, but the north- and southbound platforms looked larger than she remembered, and slightly turned around.

Looking down among the weeds and blown newspapers on the tracks, she saw a man's dress shoe. It seemed from the way it caught the sun that it might even be patent leather. Who loses a shoe? Especially a dress shoe? She looked for its mate.

The vibration inside the overpass was stronger now, building up, and then there was the overpowering, noisy pressure of a train coming from behind, from the north. It was there behind her and then it was under her and Madame S. was holding onto the railing. "Oh," she heard herself say aloud. Now she thought she should move away from the vibration, but she couldn't let go of the railing to go anywhere. She was caught. A great powerful sensation. She had to stay put, weather it. Actually, it was like weather, like getting caught in a sudden storm.

That complete, that thrilling. She could feel it in her feet, in her hands, and it traveled up through her legs and arms, the pleasure of it pressing low in her. She just had to keep her balance. It was dizzying. She tried to keep a forward spot, like the spot she held in pirouettes, but with the commotion of the train cars—everything a metal thrum, a great shaking, metal and air, strain and speed and the train passing behind and under and pushing out in front—there was nothing not moving for her to hold as a fix.

Then the train was gone. It was silent below her and Madame S. stood holding onto the railing. She wasn't sure she could let go. She didn't want to. Not quite yet.

When she could look down, Madame S. saw that the shoe hadn't been disturbed in the slightest. It was as it had been. It seemed show-offy, glinting in the sun. And by extension, the man who'd lost it. And then, there, in the turnaround, there was her pupil waving, as if Adrienne had been waiting all this time, and it was Madame S. who had been late, dillydallying. Or lost. Her old pupil was waving impatiently.

Madame S. waved back. "I'm right here," she said, without any intention of having her voice reach her pupil.

Madam S. put out her foot, testing to make sure she had her balance. There were old cracks in the cement that formed a jagged path.

She made her way down the stairs.

Her student rushed toward her, grabbing the overnight case, saying, "Hurry now. You'll be late."

"This week, everything burst into bloom," Adrienne announced as they drove through the hilly streets. "Isn't it lovely?" She said it as if Madame S. had not been kept waiting at the train station at all. As if an apology wasn't in order for leaving her alone at the station. As if Madame S. didn't have her own eyes to see how, since last Thursday, things had changed a bit. She could still feel a tremble in her stomach from the train moving under her. Despite herself, Madame S. had to admit the trees were truly something, the white dogwoods and the great bushy lilac trees posing in tiered skirts.

"The older girls have prepared something for you, Svetlana. I think you'll be surprised."

"What?" Madame S. said suspiciously, looking at her pupil and the big ring that flashed on her hand as it rode the steering wheel.

"What's the surprise, Adrienne?" She didn't want to be surprised. Not by the girls, and not by lawn after lawn costumed gorgeously in flowers.

Adrienne laughed, "Would it be a surprise it I told you? The girls would kill me."

Well, wasn't that exactly the difference, Madame S. thought, between her training and discipline and this fake school of ballet: who kills whom? The students should be afraid of the teacher, not this other way round, the teacher afraid of spoiling student fun.

"They've been working on it for weeks. You'll have to wait till after class."

The classes, there would be no surprise there. That was comforting, now, somehow. The rest seemed exhausting, the trees with that bursting vivid green and the girls with some awful late surprise. Her own body was unsettled. The girls in class might be awful but at least without surprises. These girls were like girls in villages everywhere— mild, hopeful, thick-ankled. There was no one here whose arms had a lyrical line to snap a heart.

Okay, one was a turner. One had extension but strained too hard and the leg sagged after a moment or two. Maybe one or two would travel into the city for an audition. Maybe there would even be a summer session at Harkness or Joffrey. But there would be no Budapest. Or Paris Opera. No barons. Or flowers delivered to the backstage entrance. She felt grateful for mediocrity. She didn't want to endure, didn't feel she could bear enduring these girls trying to amaze her and her having to see another new thing.

"I'm looking forward." Madame S. squinted against the dizzying proliferation of flowers and trees. It would be enough simply to keep her gaze straight ahead on the road for the rest of the ride. Adrienne was next to her, turning the wheel, talking about the end-of-the-year recital. Of course, not *Sleeping Beauty* in its entirety, condensed, but retaining the three-act structure. The parents always like something they recognize. And it was always a reliable school ballet. All the waltzes, court dances, mazurkas. A lot of chances for all levels.

"I've been working with Mary," Adrienne said. "Her Lilac Fairy is nice, still a little stiff, but we have time. That was your variation, the Lilac, wasn't it, Svetlana? One of your best. I'm sure you could dance it right now. The body doesn't forget."

From the first port de bras into the sweep of the développé à la seconde, even now Madame S. could count the measures of the Lilac Variation. She could close her eyes and feel the rigor, the elasticity and tension. But it was gone. Igor was gone. She hadn't thought of him until today. Igor who could turn like a steel rod, who had something modern and industrial about his body in motion. She had thought of him. Now he was gone. None of it was left. Even her Saint Petersburg, gone, nothing left with a grand gesture to it. Which girl? Which of these girls was Mary?

"How do I open the window?" Madame S. said. Her hand fumbled at the car door. "I need air."

Her old pupil pressed a button and the window slid down. The quick slipping of the window made Madame S. feel sicker. The vibration was still lodged in her. Something feral and excited low in her belly. She took narrow breaths, trying to maintain her gaze straight ahead.

The car turned into the church parking lot.

"We're here," her pupil said, as if Madame S. might be uncertain where they were. Two girls were rushing down the stairs. Was one of them the Mary learning the Lilac Variation? The girls were hurrying to the basement room, where class was about to begin. Madame S. could feel it had already begun.

"Are you ready, Svetlana?" Adrienne had come around to open the car door. She held out her hand. Madame S. stood from the car without help and walked briskly toward the church. The afternoon light stung her eyes. She didn't stop or wobble. She kept her balance.

There. That would be the lesson today. Not to strain, not to get behind tempo. "Abandon, but not without control," she'd say. "Close your eyes," she'd say, instructing the pianist to begin the Tchaikovsky waltz. She'd make them stand still, eyes shut, while the pianist played the piece four times. "Do you see where you are? Do you see yourself performing each step inside each note?"

She leaned on the metal railing as she managed the three steps to the basement. Through the door's small window she could see the girls at the barre, relaxed, warming up. She opened the door and they quickly adjusted their line, spaced evenly apart. The girls kept their eyes forward, chins up, feet and arms in first position.

As she did each week, Madame S. announced, "We begin. Preparation one and two."

The pianist struck the opening chords. Madame. S. walked the length of the girls and felt them tighten fearfully as she stepped near. She made her way, tapping a hand, a shoulder, adjusting a hip. She stopped at one girl and leveled her hand flat under the girl's chin.

After the barre, she asked for a long adagio. Then a couple of combinations that demanded quick footwork. "Cleaner," she insisted. "Don't mark it. Dance. This is, in fact, a dance class." She motioned with her hand to have the front line switch with the back line.

"Keep a spot. Keep a spot," she shouted curtly as the girls did piqué turns at an angle across the floor.

Finally, at the end of class, one by one, the girls curtsied. Then there was clapping.

∾

Cloth napkins, plated cutlery, everything properly situated on the dining room table. At last the dinner. Beef! A beef stew, carrots and peas and potatoes. A side salad with dressing. A warm roll on the bread plate. The pupil's husband passed Madame S. the butter and she knifed a thick pat of softened butter onto her plate. Then another. Madame S. tried not to look hungry or eat too enthusiastically.

"You really looked pleased with the girls today," the pupil said.

Madame S. nodded her head, but it was clear that response wouldn't be sufficient. She took her time chewing, then swallowed.

"You are doing well with them, Adrienne," Madame S. said. "How you've gotten that big girl actually off the ground is practically a miracle." The two women laughed.

Then Adrienne asked to hear again one of the old Bolshoi stories. Madame S. accepted a second helping. The basket of rolls came around again. Oh, those years! The years with Alexi! You can't imagine how it was for us then. Every day, a change. Thrilling! You never knew what he'd ask.

So what, she invented few details. Why not? There was plenty of food still on the table. Another roll, more butter, she was famished. The pupil's husband and daughter excused themselves. Adrienne ladled out more beef stew from the tureen. Madame S. managed slowly what was on her plate.

Adrienne could listen to stories all night. Maybe the baron didn't quite insist he bring her to the seaside villa. Maybe there weren't telegrams and bouquets of flowers waiting at every stage door. There had been someone just to care for Svetlana's costumes. An extra ovation or the evening of praise and toasts by Danka after the performance. Who was left to say otherwise? Danka, Georgi, Tamariska—Madame S. gave everyone a nickname.

"No, I have everything. I am just fine," she said when her pupil asked.

She forced herself to leave two spoonfuls of pudding in the dessert bowl. But before they stood from the dining table, she finished the pudding.

Then Madame S. went upstairs and settled onto the daughter's bed, the nice flowered coverlet folded down. The room had a bright orange-and-pink flowered wallpaper and orange wall-to-wall carpet. Madame S.'s shoes were paired on the floor, her black skirt and blouse and cardigan hung over the chair. She creamed her feet, pressing over the gnarl of bunion with her thumbs. She flexed and pointed her feet ten counts, as she did each night. Then she dangled them off the bed and beat sharply in petits battements.

She tried to kick her feet looser and sloppier, like the boy with his sneakers on the train. It was understood that for the train ride back to the city, there would be a paper bag with an apple and two sandwiches in wax paper. She'd hold back, keeping the sandwiches for Friday and Saturday supper. Then four days she would have the hunger as living proof. That brutal gratefulness she must endure. Every week there was Thursday.

MAKE ME DO THINGS

WAY OVER THERE, THE BOY COULD SEE THEM, IN THE DEEP END, HIS mother and the man his mother said he'd better stop calling Dan Dog. They were all the way over there, doing what his mother told him was the dead man's float. He could do it too, she said, no reason in the world, she said, no reason not to just swim over to the deep end and float.

"Try that I can't swim," he'd said to his mother as she bobbed away.

"Well, palley-walley, it's you who's making the big mistake," she said before she rolled over and spread out her arms.

He could see them in their sprawl, Dan Dog's legs sunk down in the water, the straps of his mother's swimsuit in a drifty signature around her.

When he saw the man lift his face up, he shouted, "Hey Dan Dog, fetch this." The man took a closed-eyed breath and lay his billowed face back down in the water.

The boy stood on the pool steps and opened his arms. He wore wings, blown-up, electric-orange wings, bunched on his arms.

"Here I go," he shouted.

He leaped. He bounced on his tiptoes till he came to the place where the bottom sloped steeply. It had a pull, he could feel it, the deep end, a suck that the boy knew wanted to get him. He doggie-paddled back to the stairs. Tucking his legs up, he kept himself down in his tuck and squatted his way up to the top step.

The man rolled on his back, his feet pointing straight up, the way the boy had seen a man float on a morning cartoon.

"Dan Dog," he shouted, singsong. "Roll over, Dan Dog."

His mother lifted her face for air, squinching open her eyes, then she dove under in a clean pike. The boy could see her below water arranging her swimsuit and he guessed she would break surface just where she broke the surface, squeezing herself up in a rush through the man's legs.

"Hey!" said the man. "What the fuck?"

His mother downed the man in a swift dunk.

"You didn't hear that, did you?" she called over to the boy. "Come on," she said. "Am I ever going to see you swim or what?"

The boy saw a pawed hand come out of the water and pull his mother under in a quick yank. She popped up, blowing water in a snorty laugh. The man popped up beside his mother, whipping her swimsuit top in a skim on the water, and the boy heard him bark into her hair, "I'm going to get you bad."

"Look at me, Dan Dog!" the boy shouted from the top step, where he stood making half flaps with his winged arms.

"Look, pal," said his mother, flattening out on her back, "what did we say about that?" She sculled in place and then did a little watery arabesque, her body folding and sinking slightly. "I haven't done all this in I don't know how many years," she said, coming back up, her shut face, the boy could see, cresting just on top of the water.

"If you throw a brand-new baby in water, it will swim," said the man. "You're making a big deal out of nothing. I mean, we're practically fish for Christ's sake," he said and tossed the strappy swim top out onto the pool deck.

"I'm not a fish, Dan Dog. Do I look like a fish?" said the boy.

The mother said, "I've got you, really," and pushed off against the side of the pool. "Trust me," she said, stretching her arms out above her head. "See, the water holds you up."

"I'm not a fish," insisted the boy.

He pulled and the nylon squeaked, stuck and sticking against the boy's wet skin before the wings came off.

They could just forget about his going in, but the boy knew they were not forgetting—the way they kept lifting their faces, calling to him to join them in the dead man's float. He would—no matter what they said to him—just not go in.

"Fine," said his mother, "be that way."

The boy was out again, doing his tiptoed best.

Whatever they said, his mother and the man, Dan Dog, the boy could feel the drain's pull. Even back here, on the shallow steps where he'd crab walked himself over to, there was the drain's suck, sucking him over to the deep end, where his mother hung on Dan Dog's back while Dan Dog did pull-ups on the diving board.

Really, it was proof, wasn't it? His furred neck, and the way he shook himself off, water spraying out just like water shook from a dog, wasn't that proof, really?

"I used to do a hundred," the man said, yanking himself up in what looked to the boy to be a motion from the same cartoon where the big bad guy had the little woman and she was holding on for her dear, good life.

His mother squealed.

"Twenty-five, twenty-six," the man yanked, "twenty-seven, twenty-fuck, twenty-shit, oh shit!" he said, letting go, and the boy watched the joined splash of his mother and the man and the sink and sunk shape of them still joined, over in the deep end.

"Oh, Dan Dog," he called. "Ruff, ruff, Dan Dog." The man was face-down in his dead man's float. His mother was floating on her back, her hands cupped and sculling close to her side. If they were dead men and dogs in the deep end, the boy wondered what that made him over in the shallow end.

"Check this out," he called, flapping his wingless arms. Then he dropped his arms and called out, "You know, I'm a human, too."

"Make me do things," said his mother.

The boy sat on the steps.

"Say anything and I'll do it—it'll be fun," the mother said. She was treading water.

The boy said, "Okay, be Mom."

The mother splashed over. "You know, you're a real pill. Come on, can we have a little fun or what? Please, just give me a thrill, just say, 'do a crab' or say, 'do the bunny breaststroke.' It will be fun, really. Okay? Please." His mother stretched out flat on her back and did a flutter kick over to where the man floated.

The boy said, "Okay, fine, be the ocean," but his mother had already rolled over into her dead man's float.

It seemed to the boy that they were hardly coming up for air—Dan Dog's back looked swollen and pink, his mother strapless and drifting slightly under—neither raising for full enough breaths and neither lifting, now, very much at all.

The boy called, "I say be an octopus," and when his mother did not stir, he said, "I'm playing. Okay, Mom, I'm playing now."

The boy walked around the edge of the pool, his bare feet pumiced by the cement. It felt good to the boy to be over here by the deep end of the pool and safe too, looking out there back to the shallow end. He saw one wing floating, orange and puffed, by the steps. The other he could not find, till he found it shored, electric, under the man's arm, black hair seaweeded thickly over it.

His mother floated right in front of him. He thought that if he just leaned over he could touch her; for good luck he might just give her a little touch; he might touch the clean, white stripe of skin on her back for extra good luck. He did it and she startled, roiled, rolling over with her legs kicking and her arms grabbing up, raising herself as his mother would in alarm. The boy was holding on to something hard of her.

"Oh, it's you," he heard her say. Then he felt the seizing undertow and knew that about his position in the animal kingdom he had been right.

RED ROOSTER

ANY IDIOT COULD HAVE TOLD HIM IT WOULDN'T WORK. PRETTY MUCH every idiot did. Starting with his own idiot ex-wife, Carine.

"What are you thinking, Dan?" she said. "You barely like your own son."

He was standing at his old front door, at his not-anymore house, where she'd installed stone lions. His not-anymore wife had put pretentious fucking lion statues on either side of his old front door.

"Ouch, that's my heart you're stabbing," Dan said with a wincing smile. Carine smiled, though Dan could see she didn't want to. Her lips opened, her real genuine-article toothy smile, not that thin-lipped bogus thing he'd watched her stretch on for photographs or in uncertain, demanding conversations. That-a-way, my man, Dan thought, you've still got some moves on her.

Carine was right, sort of at least, about the son, his son. But it wasn't so much liking him or not liking him. It was different. More particular. The boy hit nerves, like tooth pain. Like his son's way of laughing. It was annoying. Overjolly. And a lot overjolly. Like everything in life was hysterical. And the boy would actually say that. "Look at that, Dad," he'd say, pointing at a road sign: Slow Children Playing. "You see what that says! They're calling the children slow! That's hysterical!"

"I love my Danny boy," Dan said to Carine. He heard the boy coming down the stairs, bumping his rolling backpack on the wood steps. And laughing. Hysterically. Probably at the jalopying wheels, which weren't funny to Dan.

Annoying, yes.

Funny, not so much.

What Dan wasn't telling Carine was that it was easier, way easier, with the girlfriend's kid, because he didn't have to care. Nothing was personal. It wasn't really about him. If Dan paid attention. Or didn't. Not his son. It wasn't obligatory.

He'd tested that right away. Right off the bat, Dan had said Fuck. Said Shit. Didn't remind the boy to put a napkin in his lap. Didn't even look up when the kid burped at the table.

Now here was his boy, Danny, exclaiming, "Hey, hey, hey big Daddy-o," and even though Dan held open his arms and lifted his son up for their weekly ritual of knocking heads, Dan was mostly thinking, Why does he have to laugh that obnoxious laugh?

"Hey, hey, right back at you, Danny-o," Dan said, giving Danny a fast kiss on his cheek.

"I'm just telling you." Carine matched her eyes to Dan's over their son's bobbling head, her lips thinned to the hateful line. "I'm just here telling you. It won't work."

Last night, actually even before Carine, it was the girlfriend.

He liked the word *girlfriend* so much. Out loud, he called her Juliana or Jules, but in his mind he always called her the girlfriend.

"I'm not sure," the girlfriend said, before she'd even made it down the full flight of stairs and poured herself a big glass of the fancy-ass white wine she liked to drink, and drink a little quickly for Dan's taste. He could still hear the boy crying, not the wail he'd kept up at an Olympic fucking level for a gold medal record of two hours. Now it was a simpery, needy mewling.

"You tell me, how we can ever make this work?" the girlfriend said.

The girlfriend looked frazzled from her kid's tantrum. Hair messy, disheveled T-shirt, so nerve-fried she looked flushed and drained in the face at the same time. She looked as though she'd been picked up in the tantrum, tossed and splintered like a wood house in a tornado. He felt concerned for her, not exactly in a doctorly way but not without a measure of clinical distance.

Dan felt an easy hum in his brain. It was crazy how easy it was, another person's kid. It didn't even matter that this kid had a major decibel range. It just didn't tear up his heart the way Danny's crying did. Didn't tear or scratch or piss him off or make him want to bash a door or break glasses or take the fucking kid and throttle him silent. It didn't make Dan feel inadequate. Weirdly, it made him feel good. Sexy good. Like he could bone the girlfriend till she had nothing left to worry about, and do it right there, by her fancy stainless steel fridge, where she was reaching in and pulling out the corked Pinot Grigio.

He felt invincible.

"It will, Jules," Dan said. "I can make anything work," and he rolled a little bicep curl and then pumped it Popeye-after-spinach-style. Fuck yeah. He could match that kid's Olympic tantrum with Olympic patience.

❧

"What?" Danny said. They were in the car, coming back from errands. Dan barely had errands, but whatever he did have he saved to have something to do with Danny on their days. It worked to have a routine. Today: dry cleaner, lightbulbs, bubble wrap, wrench, groceries. Then minigolf: winner got the Super Brownie Shake. They always ate the Rooster Burgers and shared an order of large fries.

Dan didn't have many chores either, but he saved garbage, re-cycling, laundry, vacuuming for weekends with Danny. Once, Dan'd left his icebox open just so they could defrost it. It was important to teach the boy something about feeling invested in a home. Even if Dan half wished the home he once owned would catch on fire and burn to the ground with the fucking guard lions still in place. Even a rental apartment like this, even a tent in the woods, Dan explained to his son, needs sweeping once in awhile.

"What what?" Dan said. He heard *pop pop pop*. Danny had got-ten into the roll of bubble wrap. "Awesome," Danny had said when his father took it off the hardware shelf. "What's it for?"

"Wrapping stuff," Dan answered in a tone meant to end the discussion.

"Not this, the whatever it was Mom said back at home." Danny said, his hands working steadily over the plastic. It made Dan's neck tighten, each plastic pop.

"I don't know what you're talking about," Dan said. But he did, of course he did. This was an example of what was easier about the girlfriend's kid. He didn't have to explain anything. Come up with good reasons. Make plans. Make the future right. Teach the right lesson. Fuck, he barely had to look at the kid during a meal. Even if the kid spilled his soda. And fuck, sure, let the kid have two sodas. It wasn't Dan's dentist bill.

"All in good time, Danny-o," Dan said. They'd been driving in silence. Or a silence irritated by bubble wrap pops.

"All in good time, that's what I tell them all," he repeated when his son hadn't followed up with the "What what Daddy-o?" that Dan had expected. He wouldn't tell his son much, just talk loosely about change and rolling with change. That if you were with the people you loved, everything worked out fine. Or maybe he wouldn't say that last line, since if you gave that a two-second pause, it appeared a pretty flawed line of reasoning in Danny's life.

"I think it's all going to work out for us," Dan said. He looked over and saw his son, staring straight ahead, his small hands working along the rows of plastic, feeling for a stray air-filled cushion.

A car careened into Dan's lane and Dan gave it on the horn a little longer than necessary. Usually that would get a rise from Danny, like putting on the horn was a you-get-'em sign of his dad's strength. But Danny was squinting, focused on the road. Dan didn't think his kid could keep quiet that long, even in sleep.

"I know exactly what's what," Danny said suddenly, with one of his weird hiccupy laughs and then kept up a droning of *what what what what what* like a syncopated beat against the bubble wrap.

Dan turned in under a red-and-white cutout rooster. Red Rooster, it said in letters that hung from the rooster's talons. He looked for his girlfriend's car and felt juiced seeing she'd parked just where he'd instructed her to park, under the trees by the picnic tables. "One thing at a time," he told her, after she'd had her second glass of wine and he'd led her to her velvet couch, giving her a serious round of I-believe-you-need-this-fucking. "Accidentally the first time, then a few planned times and by the end of month the boys will be begging for us to move in together." She looked at him with what Dan thought was postfuck gratefulness. "Whatever you say, boss."

Dan had kissed her half-closed eyes. "Now you're talking like my kind of modern woman."

"I'm definitely winning today," Dan said. He pulled in and parked a couple cars away from the girlfriend's car. "I've got the winner's feeling today." He said this every time he and Danny arrived at minigolf. He did not believe in allowing his son to win just because he was a kid. What kind of lesson was that?

"I'm already trying to decide between strawberry or a black-and-white Super Brownie Shake," Dan said.

"Okay, you win. Do we have to play?" Danny said in a flat, petulant voice. Dan saw that his son had not even looked up.

"And what kind of question's that?" Dan could see his girlfriend and her kid over by the picnic benches. They were sitting on a table, their feet resting on the plank bench. They were working on ice cream cones. Large chocolate-and-vanilla-twist cones. He watched them turning the cones, in matching rhythm. She'd gotten it wrong. They'd done it backward. Play first, then the boys get lunch. Game then reward. Didn't it seem like the obvious order? If she was counting on him making a plan that could work, then why couldn't she listen to something that simple? Especially this, the first meeting, doing it accidental-style. It wasn't a fucking disaster in his larger plan. He'd adjust. But what was with her?

"Well, hey, hey, hey, look at that." Dan opened the car door.

"There's a lady I'm friends with. This lady and her kid."

The boy didn't look up. "Where?"

Dan pointed. "He's okay. Not you, doesn't hold a candle to you, but he's not a psycho or anything."

"I'm sure," Danny said.

Dan went first to eliminate the question of which boy got to go first.

"That's so unfair," the kid said, pulling on Juliana. "You said I could go first, Mom."

Dan leaned over his putter. Dan heard her say, "Yes, Tracey, but now we're playing with another family."

"Why?" the kid hissed.

Dan felt focused. It didn't matter what her kid said; it never mattered. Tracey, he mostly even forgot that was the kid's name. It was a weird name. For a boy. Tracey. But that wasn't his business either. Then Danny said, "Welcome to my dad; he always goes first."

Dan felt his back go tense. What did that mean? What the fuck? And since when? When, actually, Dan always let Danny whine his way into going first. Dan closed his eyes, adjusted his stance, and tried to breathe into the spasm he could feel shooting from his neck down his arm. Then he opened his eyes and took a stroke. It made a clean line through the hole in the lighthouse.

"Hole in one," he said, looking over at his son.

The fifth hole, the windmill, was deceptively hard.

"That's four," the girlfriend said, pulling the pencil from behind her ear. She was scorekeeper. It was just like her to take her job so seriously. Yes, Dan had done it on four hits. But it was kind of fucked up, since it was obvious he should have had it on the third. It was kind of Danny's fault because Danny wouldn't shut up even though he knew his dad's rule. Talking was fine between holes. Not during.

"Hey," Dan said, "cut the chitchat."

"Come on," said the girlfriend. "Are we playing a game or are we playing the Masters?"

He heard Danny laugh.

The girlfriend laughed conspiratorially. "So I see your dad gets a little competitive?"

"Tracey," Dan said, standing just behind where the boy was readying to swing. "On your third breath hit the ball and you'll avoid the windmill." The boy shot Dan a look. Dan realized he'd never called the kid by his name. "That's right, Tracey, your third breath, Tracey."

The boy knocked the ball and it slid right through the rotating sails of the windmill. He ran to the other side and easily downed the ball on his second hit. "Look at that!" the kid shouted, "I did in two. That's better than you."

"You bet, Tracey," Dan said. He felt affection surge, uncomplicated.

Then it was Danny's turn, but Danny was standing on one foot, hopping to keep balance. "This is too easy," he said. He hopped and swung and the ball whacked right into a wooden sail, ricocheting into the gravel. Danny hopped over and picked up the ball, all on one foot. He hopped back, gravel slipping and crunching under his jumps. "Somebody's got to do something to make this boring game interesting."

Tracey was laughing. He began jumping on one leg. Juliana was laughing. Dan half expected her to start jumping up and down too.

"Can you just play," said Dan. The girlfriend came close to Dan while Danny kept up his hopping. He hit and the ball bounced off the windmill again.

"This is stupid, Danny." Dan said.

"Please, Dan," the girlfriend spoke quietly. "They're having fun. That's what we want, right?"

"There are rules," Dan said and walked off to wait at the sixth hole, where there was a large white rooster sporting a red bow tie. The rooster had a hand on one hip and a kicked-out leg. There was a hole in the rooster's big white tennis shoe where the golf ball had to pass through.

Dan tried hard not to look back at his son, who he could hear was keeping up the one-foot shenanigans.

"Danny, try whacking it on your third breath," Tracey said and it was Tracey who counted a slow one, two, three. Dan kept himself from looking. He heard the *thwonk* when the club connected with the ball, then Tracey shouting, "How cool is that? That's what your dad taught me."

Dan turned and saw Danny hopping to finish up his shot, his head practically sliced by the turning windmill. The ball had landed at the lip of the hole. Danny tapped it in.

"Can we make my score two? Please?" Danny asked Juliana, excitedly. "I didn't know the windmill trick until Tracey told me."

"That's fair," Juliana said. "Anyway, we're making the rules." She balanced the score sheet on her knee.

Dan set up his ball and took a practice swing.

"Fair as in completely unfair," Dan called at the girlfriend. "As in nothing to do with the game of minigolf. But what the fuck do I know?" He wanted to start in on the rooster hole. It was bad form, against the rules, but hey, wasn't everyone else ready to do whatever suited them best?

"Dad! Dad!" Danny shrieked, jumping now on both legs. "You cursed! You cursed!"

"Are you kidding, your dad curses all the time," Tracey said. "At my house he's a major curser."

"He's at your house?" Danny said, as if he were exposing a big lie. "When?"

"Hey, it's my turn," Juliana said quickly. "Can someone pay attention? I am having a hole-in-one feeling."

Super Brownie Shakes all around because, of course—wasn't it obvious?—the girlfriend decided everyone was a winner. Dan saw that Danny had gone pouty, his shake pretty much untouched. Hysterical or pouty, sometimes it seemed that was his son's whole emotional range. It probably didn't help that Tracey was leaning in, telling Danny how he'd figured out the angle and next time he'd definitely get a hole in one on the last crazy-maze hole.

"It's actually super easy," Dan heard the kid say. It wasn't easy. Even though the kid was right that working the ball to ricochet off the left-corner wood block was exactly the way to play the maze hole. One game of minigolf and Tracey had figured that out. How many Saturdays had he brought Danny to the Red Rooster and still Danny had no strategy, hitting the ball every ridiculous which way.

Under the picnic table, the girlfriend pressed her leg against Dan. It was warm and Dan could almost feel the tan she'd been devoted to deepening for the last month. He liked the way her browned skin looked, especially the contrasting white triangles on her breasts. But it was reckless, really, that tan. Didn't she listen to all the caution about the sun? Dan worked at his burger. Tracey stood, showing Danny some kind of hand-and-song game. Danny still looked mopey but he was, even sluggishly, doing the grip and high five and front-back paddywhack moves that Tracey was teaching him.

"I think it's going pretty good," the girlfriend said.

"Well," Dan said. Neither boy had finished their burgers. Dan had a rule with Danny, an obvious finish first, then play.

"Well what?" she said.

"Pretty well. Not good. I think it's going pretty well."

She knocked her leg this time against his. Hard. Harder again. "You can be an asshole. Like, a really serious asshole," she whispered, covering her face from the boys with her brownie shake.

Now Tracey was teaching Danny songs for the hand-clap game.

"That's it," Tracey encouraged. "Let's do it again." Dan couldn't believe they were the same idiotic songs he remembered from his school playground, the girls chanting, *Miss Mary Mack Mack Mack, all dressed in black black black*, crossing arms, hitting thighs, then clapping hands three times. When did boys start playing these games? That's just what Dan needed, Tracey teaching his boy a bunch of girl games and his already loosey-goosey Danny would grow loosier and goosier, and never even make it to sign up for something as boy-solid as Little League.

Then Tracey was taking Danny the second time through another song-and-clap game Dan vaguely remembered. *Miss Lucy had a steamboat the steamboat had a bell Miss Lucy went to heaven and the steamboat went to HELL O operator give me number nine and if you disconnect me I will kick you in the BEHIND the fridgerator there was a piece of glass Miss Lucy sat upon it and it went right up her ASK me no more questions . . .*

The boys were excited, slowing, then shouting at the almost bad words. Danny was more than shouting; he was screaming. Top of his lungs.

Hysterically, Dan thought.

"Whoa, whoa boys," Dan said. "Do you think we're the only ones here?"

The boys didn't slow down, let alone quiet down. It seemed Danny had gotten even louder. Danny spun in on another round of the game.

"Whoa," Dan repeated. "That's not okay."

"You curse; we curse," Danny said. He didn't even look over at his dad.

"That's enough, Danny-o; we're out of here." Dan's voice was harsh, unbending. They had things to do. Errands. He wanted to be alone with his son.

The boys stopped. They looked stricken in a way that pleased Dan. That's the way. Sometimes a little parental enforcement was necessary.

"Can Danny come to our house?" Tracey asked in a whine that bordered on begging. "Please?"

"Please, Dad," Danny repeated. Then Danny was jumping, two feet this time and Tracey was jumping too, both boys shouting, "please please please please please please," as they jumped around the picnic table. And just as Dan was saying, "Another time, boys. There will be another—" the girlfriend was saying, "Hey, you kids really get along. This is great. Sure Danny, we'd love to have you. Should we include your grumpy old dad on this playdate?"

∾

Dan couldn't remember having ever actually agreed, but here he was, driving toward the girlfriend's house. The best he could claim was having put his foot down about Danny riding in her car. "No, I'll take Dan. His mom's a little picky about his going off in other people's cars." Dan knew it was kind of a low blow. First, relying on Carine's cautiousness. Second, calling the girlfriend *other people*. But he wanted to be in charge. He thought the girlfriend wanted him to be in charge. Of this, doing the "blending," as the books optimistically called what now felt more like tossing than blending. Suddenly, everyone all together for an afternoon felt fast. Reckless, Dan thought, maybe this is all a little reckless.

"She could be your girlfriend, Dad," Danny said, as soon as they pulled out of the Red Rooster. "I like her and she could be your girlfriend. Don't you think?"

A car and then another car cut in front of him. Juliana's car went through the yellow light but it was red by the time Dan came to the stoplight.

"Whoa, Danny-o. Don't you think that's a little fast? You just met Tracey's mom."

"Yeah, but I like Tracey. If they have a cool house, we could move there. You've been there? Is the house cool? We could have a TV show about us. You two could get married on the show and Tracey and I would do stuff and everything and it would be cool. Don't you think?"

Dan looked at his son. The boy looked desperate, and Dan felt that he was seeing for the first time just how reckless the last couple years had been. He couldn't count how many times he'd claimed that the whole damaging-cost-on-the-kid argument was way overrated. He'd liked telling people that Danny claimed two homes were better than one because it meant two sets of Christmas presents. But now, all of Danny's jolly laughing seemed like the hysterical crust over a havoc chasm. It made Dan miss Carine and all their predictable arguments.

It made Dan want a do-over.

"I think you're jumping a couple steps ahead in the game, son." He'd never called Danny *son* before, but he liked the word's solidity, the possessive connection of the word to *father*. Like just saying it set an example. Like it set things on a corrective path.

The light went green. The girlfriend's car was nowhere in sight. Frankly, it was a little inconsiderate, zooming off like that. Did she have to go all NASCAR on him? Anyway, it made Dan glad to have his son safely belted in his car. Dan thought about turning into the next shopping center and telling Danny they had to get back and start in on their regular errands.

"Wow, you think everything is a game. Hello, I'm talking real life, Dad," Danny said in a whispery voice Dan had never heard before.

The boys were out in the yard, taking turns twisting up the tire swing rope and letting it spin out. Then they took to one boy twisting it up and quickly jumping to share the tire with the other boy. The tire swung fast. The boys shrieked, screaming out cowboy and cops-and-robbers commands, though it was unclear if they were chasing or being chased. Dan couldn't remember ever watching his son play this hard with another kid. Certainly never this well. Usually, Dan watched Danny trying to fit into the games other kids set up, but he was always awkward and bad at finding a way in. Most times Danny just made up his own games and insisted they could only be played alone.

"This is amazing," Jules said, coming around to Dan's side of the patio table. She poured them both refills of white wine. "You were right and I was an idiot worrying about it not working. I think we're all going to be okay."

The boys were tangled on the rope swing, clinging to each other's limbs. When the tire spun it was practically impossible to tell which boy was which.

"They kind of look like brothers," the girlfriend said and leaned against Dan.

"Don't you think we should cool it on the wine?" Dan said.

"Relax, baby," she said. "This is good. The boys are good. We couldn't ask for better."

He looked at the girlfriend. She looked a little smeary. Her face was slightly sunburned, probably from playing minigolf in the high sun. It seemed funny the way she never used any protection. She boasted she was born for the sun, this was peasant stock skin bred thick for working the fields. Dan could see lines by her eyes and upper lip. Great, peasant skin, peasant mentality. Not a lot of caution. Clearly, not a lot of thinking ahead.

"I'm just saying," Dan said.

"What?" She squinted. "What would that be?"

"We're the parents, right?"

"Exactly," said the girlfriend, taking a big gulp of wine. "And you're obviously really working hard today, Dan, to model maturity and accommodation."

Now Tracey showed Danny how he could do the Grand Kazizmo leap off the tire while it was still spinning. When Tracey threw himself off, there was a point when it looked to Dan like the kid's body stuck in the air. Then the kid unstuck and was crashing down, rolling off in a limb-smacking tumble. When he came to a stop, he wasn't moving. Then Tracey popped up and shook himself off like it was no biggie. Danny was shouting, "You're psycho," over and over. It was a stupid move but Dan couldn't help but think it was the exact kind of stupid move he loved showing off with as a kid. He'd basically spent his whole childhood shouting, "Look at this," as he threw himself out of trees or off cliffs into dark lakes.

"Tracey," the girlfriend screamed, "do you have to break my heart?" Dan saw she looked less frightened than proud of her kid's daring. Before, he'd thought the girlfriend was relaxed in a good, un-Carine kind of up-tight way. Now she just seemed sloppy, a little zoned out. Carine would have been stone-cold horrified.

"You do the Grand Kazizmo," Tracey shouted over to Danny. "It's crazy fun."

"It's kind of too crazy," Danny said. "I mean, maybe later." Danny shot a quick look at his dad. Dan thought he should feel good, to have a kid with a head on his shoulders, not ready to wind up in the Emergency with a broken arm or a head busted off his shoulders. Dan should give a that's-my-boy-using-his-noggin two thumbs up. But he just felt sad.

"That was something, Tracey," Dan said instead, refusing to meet his son's look. "Want me to super-duper twist you up?"

Tracey leaped back on the swing, crouching high on the tire. He perched like a squirrel while Dan made his way slowly over to the rope swing. He took his time, sheriff-style, pacing his steps cockily across the lawn. The girlfriend was saying, "Do we have to do this?" but Dan could feel that easiness, that no-worries in her voice. Egging him on. No, it was more than that, she was happy to have Dan finally paying a little attention to her kid. It was clear to Dan that if this was going to be his yard, he had to make it his yard. Dan wound the rope, coiling it higher and tighter than the boys could get it coiled. He could feel his son lurking, watching. The rope, rough, bristled against Dan's fingers. "You want it super fucking fast?" Dan whispered to Tracey. Tracey squealed and nodded and Dan whispered the question again.

"Hey, Danny-o, come help your dad," he said, turning to see where Danny had pinned himself against a tree. "Get over here, son," Dan said and felt that solidity again just from saying the word. It worked too; his son must have felt it. Danny slunk over til he was standing close to his father.

"Wanna see how it works?" Dan said.

"What?" his son said, so quietly it almost didn't seem like a question.

"The whole thing," and the father let the rope go.

ON EARTH

"WHAT IF WE WERE THE LAST ONES ON EARTH?" HER DAUGHTER SAID AFTER Sasha turned off the bedside lamp and put the book back on the shelf.

"That's not a bedtime question, buckaroo," Sasha said, leaning to press her lips against her daughter's cheek. Ella's cheek in the dark seemed softer than at any other time of day, the skin almondy from bath soap.

"But what about the dinosaurs?" Ella said, holding Sasha's arm. Dinosaurs were the new craze. Before, it had been fairies. She'd begged Sasha for the yellow wings they'd seen in the store. Then mermaids. Now it was everything *Tyrannosaurus Rex*. Everything *Pterodactyl*. Sasha was not prepared for her daughter's obsession with dinosaurs. Wasn't that a boy thing? Dump trucks, superheros, dinosaurs—what the morning coffee group called basic male destiny.

What was it with men and their end-of-the-world questions?

This afternoon, the lover had moved Sasha over to the window. "Look out there," he'd said, positioning her against the sill as he pressed into her. "We're all that's left."

"Ella, dinosaurs were hardly the last ones." Sasha kept her voice easy and matter-of-fact. "There are new species evolving on Earth all the time." That sounded right; she was pretty certain that it was right. But if it got down to particulars, Sasha couldn't whip out the name of a newly discovered Amazonian insect or hybrid amphibian. Always risky to give new information before sleep. A comment like that could keep Ella up asking questions, calling Sasha back and back and back into the room. Best she could do then was angle for a morning research project. Better yet, by morning her daughter would be on to a new obsession.

"But what about the very last dinosaurs? Did the very, very last know they were the last?"

"Roll over, my beauty," Sasha said.

Ella squiggled onto her stomach and Sasha worked her hand in small circles, the nightgown's thin cotton bunching and slipping as she moved down the delicate ridge of her daughter's spine. Sasha closed her eyes and worked to keep her breath and her hand slow, as if leading Ella to sleep by example.

"Did they?" Ella's voice pushed up. There again, that urgent, worried thread. Not just a fear of extinction, but the sorrow of the final one, the one that endures and knows it is the very end.

Sasha worked two slow breaths, holding back from giving a response.

"I don't know about the very last," Sasha said when Ella asked again. "But I promise we're good here for a while."

"I thought she'd taken you as her prisoner," the husband said. "I was debating if you were worth the ransom." He was wiping down the kitchen counter. The room had a cleaned-up, lemon smell. He snapped the dishcloth against the air, motioning her to come close.

"I guess I should be thankful she's not pirate crazy," Sasha said and stood just behind her husband. He smelled like himself. She looked over his shoulder. His movements had so much precision and force, as if the day hadn't depleted him at all. He'd refilled their wine glasses, left them on the scrubbed countertop. The dishes were stacked precariously by the sink. It surprised her, always, how many bowls and plates and pans and pots were used to feed just three of them. The aftermath of dinner made dinner seem like a bigger meal than the one she'd prepared.

"I hate dinosaurs, Richard," Sasha said.

Her husband stretched the damp cloth over the lip of the sink. "Don't hate on dinosaurs; they roamed the good earth." Richard reached his arms behind himself to pull her against him. His hands were damp. She fit her face in the familiar place between his shoulder blades.

"Which basically means extinction is now our family's number-one leading topic of conversation," she said.

"We can manage that for her," he said. "We've managed worse. Can't we manage that, Sasha," he said, less question than fact. They were quiet then, in the kitchen. The last of everything done that needed doing. She thought it must be the same for her husband, going over that full list he needed to get through each day, making sure he'd taken care to leave nothing that would wake and then keep him up, buzzing peskily until dawn. She could feel their daughter awake in her room, worrying over the list of dinosaurs. But she wasn't calling for Sasha; that was evolution.

In the mornings after drop-off, alone or in clusters, the mothers gathered in a café. The café owner seemed pleased to have the women stick around nursing a coffee for as long as they wanted to stay. *Crack of Dawn Saloon,* one woman suggested they rename the café. "At least it sounds as if we're doing something wild," she said. Another said, "I'd vote for the *Summit*, for all that gets organized here." Neither name stuck, and most mornings a mother asked Sasha, "Coming to the Muffin?"

"What's on your plate for today?" Sasha joked with a mother in line, but another woman wearing a suit jumped in, saying, "Basically making my family's life possible."

Sasha actually thought the *Summit* was a good name, the way the mothers settled into the mismatched tables and chairs and got right to business. There was the question of a permission slip. Which trip? The orchard? Post office? Who'd figured out what was needed for the presentation? Some costume. But what costume?

"Another bedsheet I'll be dying colonial brown at eleven at night," a woman said. Another chimed in that she had two from last year; she'd bring them tomorrow.

They covered new concerns. A child's night terrors. Another's reading scores. A violin teacher's phone number was written on a napkin. There was a foiled tenth-anniversary dinner because—wouldn't you know it?—both kids spiked fevers a half hour before the reservation. Tenth, that's silver? Silver? No, bullets. Vibrators. Please, just a prescription for Ambien.

Sasha let her eyes shut and listened to the alternating hilarity and concern. She opened her eyes and, there it was, the everyday comfort of the everyday, something she thought she'd never get enough of. But this morning, as on the other Tuesdays these last two months, Sasha was the first to finish her coffee.

"Where you running off to?" a mother asked when Sasha stood from the table. "Will you be at pick-up?"

"Like, duh." Sasha mimicked the exasperated tone the kids used. "Am I ever not?"

"You shouldn't lie to your kid," the lover said. "I wouldn't ever lie to my kid."

"You don't have a kid." Sasha disentangled her leg from his, snugging the sheet around her. "You have no idea what you'd do."

"Leave it to us and we'll wreck the planet for every last creature," he said. "Forget our species' survival; there's no assurance the planet can survive our insanity."

He propped himself up on his arm and perched over her. She felt him wind up, his eyes squinching down, fixed and distant. No stopping it. The old diatribe about how we weren't worthy of having these elaborate brains, the way man had made such sorry use of his brain if the best thing he'd thought up was plastic—which, thanks, had pretty well choked off the oceans and killed God knows how much marine life, since man basically knew only how to make shit and not how to clean it up.

She looked at the lover, the squint lines around his eyes. Let him tirade away. She was drifty and satisfied and happy to look at the angle of his neck. The smooth scoop and muscle. The afternoon light on his skin. It was pretty. He was pretty in a rugged way. In the same rugged way as her husband, really. But she'd never want the lover as a husband. Too destructive. Too anarchical. This one had not learned to live in groups. Wasn't that why she was here these Tuesdays, to hide out in his outlaw, cockeyed moral code? The lover was her first lover. She had not been looking. Sometimes coming to this room felt like weather she'd inadvertently been pushed out into.

He railed on. They'd get what they deserved. *They.* There it was, that go-to turn in his argument. *They.* As if he really thought he was his own special species. Sasha'd learned she could squint down her hearing so she was not really listening to the what of what he said. Just enough for her to say, "Don't get me started on men." That would stop him. Or redirect him, at least, long enough for Sasha to turn things in a direction she wanted for the rest of her afternoon, which included his wrestling her legs under his.

"You got a problem with men?" he said, pinning her hands. "I'll show you a male problem, little missy."

When she stood to leave, the lover held out a book. "I picked this up for Ella at a used book store. It's comprehensive."

"It's way above her head," Sasha said. The book was thick with renderings of dinosaur fossils.

"Don't underestimate Ella," the lover said. "She's a smart kid."

"Quiz me," Ella said.

Jurassic, Mesozoic. Cenozoic. Where did Cretaceous fit? And there were uppers and lowers. Of all of them? Was that necessary?

Sasha needed Ella to understand that these weren't hundreds of thousands but hundreds of millions of years, but Ella said, "Well, obviously." Ella had the ages memorized and fifty different dinosaurs.

"There are at least nine hundred more," she told Sasha. "Actually, even more. But some have been reclassified."

Reclassified, kingdom, phylum. Little professor with her new words, methodical and serious, standing in front of Sasha, her arms zippered to her sides, her fairy wings bent and turned into those of a flying reptile.

"Quiz me more," she said.

"Okay, start with the nice ones," Sasha said, looking at the list in the large book. She'd told Ella the book was from a used book store, which wasn't exactly a lie.

"Aeolosaurus. Herbivore. Guessed to be as big as forty-five feet. Not to be confused with Allosaurus. Predator. Pretty much the worst bad guy. Bipedal." Ella spoke quickly in staccato bursts, as if she needed to get it all out in a single breath. "Then there's Barosaurus and Bactrosaurus." She took big in-and-out, stalling breaths, her face furrowed. "Give me a hint for another," she said, looking away from her mother.

"Big horns on the head," Sasha said. "Scared of Rex."

"Triceratops! Triceratops! Triceratops!" Ella shouted.

"That's right."

"I know." Ella sounded bored, as if her mother's enthusiasm was beneath the rigorous inquiry. "The Sauropods could be one hundred fifty feet long. The mothers laid dozens of eggs because the odds of survival were so small."

"Just another reason to be glad I'm human" Sasha said and shut the big book.

Her husband lifted Sasha to take her in his mouth. She pressed her hands against the wall and leaned so that he could only graze her. She could manage the pressure this way.

"Richard." She said her husband's name, and he said something into her that might have been her name. She held herself off until she couldn't, and Richard, feeling her shift, kept at her, pressing with his hand now too, so she wouldn't turn back.

Later, he asked about her day.

"Pretty much, I'm living in the Jurassic," Sasha said.

He ran his hand up her leg. "I'm glad you're not one of the armored beasts."

"I just have no armor left," she said. "What are we living in now?"

"It's the Holocene," Richard said without pausing. "Actually, there's a bit of a movement to name this geological period Anthropocene, acknowledging post-industrial-age human impact."

His voice was absorbed, brimming, always prepared. Was there any subject he couldn't speak about with some intelligence? She counted on this voice, Richard's knowing, quiet and steady in the dark. Even when she shouldn't have counted on his voice, she did.

"Well, it's obvious this dinosaur thing is bred in the bone." Sasha poked her hip against his leg.

"It could be worse. It could have been spider DNA."

"Arachnophobia?" And she readied for what fast response he'd ping-pong back at her.

"No, simply a penchant for hiding in silky undergarments. On one side of my family it led to males sporting women's brassieres. That branch didn't do well in reproducing."

Sasha thought if she told the women in the Muffin about the lover, they would be surprised most of all that she had no complaint about her husband. Was there anything better than this, lying in the familiar dark with her husband, delighted by everything he said? With one, she never thought very much about the other. She'd thought that it would be different, that she'd compare or get confused who was who. But maybe no one would be surprised. Maybe each of the women she had coffee with each morning kept a secret just so they had a place outside the known limit. A protection against disaster. Maybe especially the husband would understand.

On the train to the city, Ella sat with her face pressed to the window. "What's that?" she asked, her breath fogging the glass. "What's that?" And each time when Sasha said, "What?" Ella said, "Too late. It's gone."

When the train swept into the tunnel before the station, her daughter wriggled on her coat.

"We've got a bit," Sasha said. "You'll get overheated."

The conductor came over the system and in a scratchy voice announced their arrival.

"We've got to go. Let's go. Get your coat on, Mom." There was something frantic in Ella's voice that reminded Sasha of the way she felt as a girl when a shopkeeper said the store was closing. Sasha's mother would tease, "Trust me. No one's going to make us sleep here."

"Sweet potato, what's the hurry? The museum's not going anywhere."

Ella looked at Sasha, so disappointed that her mother couldn't understand the obvious. "This is going to be the most important day of my life." Ella stood up from the train bench.

"I'm going to be Louis Leakey," Ella said. Sasha took her daughter's hand and felt envy at that much certainty.

Mothers alone. Babysitters in a knot of strollers. Coats shed on the ground. Boys circled the monumental skeletons.

Little hunters, Sasha thought. But where were the girls? Had they all run off to the butterfly conservatory, with its moist environment, layers of bird trills and chirps piped in? It was called hatching, what butterflies did: the caterpillar wrapping into a silky button, becoming a pupa, the chrysalis hanging by a soft sling, then breaking for the butterfly to spill out. Somehow all those transformations sounded female to Sasha.

She should take Ella to the gift shop and find one of those home kits for a butterfly garden.

Sasha located Ella standing under a Diplodocus, staring up at the vast curve of its massive neck. Ella's lips moved. Sasha moved close and heard Ella reciting facts.

Then Ella led Sasha to a wall placard that explained theories of extinction and asked her mother to read the information.

"You read to me," Sasha said, but her daughter shook her head.

"Mom, just read. I need to concentrate."

Sasha read, silently prepared to summarize.

"Don't skip anything," Ella said. "Every date. Even the names of the scientists."

There was the climate change theory. The shifting of temperatures and the shifting makeup of the atmosphere. Twelve times more carbon dioxide. More oxygen. Eventually, the respiratory systems could not cope. There was the theory in which a huge asteroid landed in what we now know as Mexico, causing climate changes.

Ultimately, each theory came down to a failure to adapt to changing conditions.

"But extinction wasn't an absolute," Sasha was happy to read. "Birds, for example, are believed to have evolved from certain feathered dinosaurs."

"But a lot didn't turn into birds," Ella said. "They just died."

Then she was off again, circling through the room, stopping in front of each large fossil. Sasha watched Ella watching two boys who pretended to slay dinosaurs.

"I want to go." Her daughter was suddenly holding Sasha's coat sleeve, tugging. "This place is stupid."

"What happened?" Sasha looked around the high-ceilinged room for what had gone awry.

Ella refused to answer, even after they had made their way down two flights of stairs, passed the gift shop, and were out on the street.

"That was for kids, Mom," she finally said.

"Okay."

"You don't get it, do you? Louis Leakey would have hated that place."

"She should have better heroes," the lover said. "Did you tell her Leakey had an affair in the first year of marriage? Knocked her up. Left the wife. Then basically robbed Africa right and left for his own glory."

"Leakey's a hero. He devoted his life to Africa." Sasha regretted having said anything as soon as she'd said it. She'd just finished reading Ella a book on Louis Leakey. They'd stayed up later than bedtime, lost in the dangers and dust of excavations. Sasha liked the Leakey book because it favored evolution over extinction. When they finished the book, Ella announced that she'd bring her parents to the field the way Leakey took his family.

"Are you joking, *Africa*? He devoted his life to the fucking cult of Louis Leakey," the lover said. He was up, pacing the small apartment. "His wife found fossils and he fucked other women. He was fucking competitive with his own kids. Real fucking hero material."

He looked feral in his own home, his long, bare legs gliding from one wall to the next. "Sasha, you'd do better giving Ella the biography of Emma Goldman or Margaret Sanger."

"Margaret Sanger? You really don't have a clue. Ella's seven," Sasha said. Sasha counted four steps, and then he pivoted and walked in a new direction.

"Let's go out for food," he'd said, turning suddenly to face Sasha.

She'd only seen him a few times out of the room, and those before he'd become the lover. It was only two months ago that she'd first seen him at a bookstore's cash register, holding two books in the air, arguing with the owner about civil liberties. She couldn't remember how he'd seemed to her then, but now she couldn't imagine him managing city streets. He'd be the kook banging a fist against cars he thought too big. Would he deign to stop at crosswalks?

"I might be crazy coming here, but I'm not an idiot," she said.

"What's the big deal?" he'd said. "You never walk with anyone in public?"

What could she say back? She refused to say he wasn't just *anyone*. She didn't want to say the truth, which was that she really only walked in the world with other women. Other women and their children. Or her husband and their daughter.

"Well, I'm out of here," he said. "I haven't been out in days." He was into his clothes; his fingers rumpled through his hair. She sat on his bed and watched.

"Come with me, my love," he said with a theatrical bow, but he turned before she could even shake her head.

"I'll bring us back food," he shouted when he was outside the door.

She could hear his feet, fast, jumping two steps at a time. The metal door banged shut. Then it was quiet. She had never been alone in the lover's room. With him there, the room with its low bed and desk and eating table seemed like a hideaway, a place out of time, but with him gone, Sasha saw the room for what it was—a crummy rental where a middle-aged man lived and would likely live until he could no longer be called middle-aged.

She counted seven steps from the bed to the refrigerator and five from the bed to the desk. There were three orderly stacks of files and papers on the desk. She looked through his bills. He owed less than two hundred dollars on his credit card, the prior month paid in full. She looked at the charges. Small charges. Never more than twenty-five dollars. How was that possible? Her life with Richard and their daughter was a hemorrhage of money each month. When she'd look up from writing checks and say to Richard, "We better do something to stop this," he'd say she was wrong. "We can manage, Sasha," he'd say. They were doing something good, he'd remind her, and that would be making a life.

The refrigerator was two steps beyond grim. A couple bowls of starchy pasta. A metal takeout container with rice stuck on the paper lid. There were juice cartons with the spouts open, and Sasha imagined him standing in the sour light of the open refrigerator, drinking straight from the carton. Sasha took a big gulp and felt something clumpy slip down her throat. The ceiling had cracks; plaster and paint hung in shavings where a leak had dried. Before, she'd been grateful for that ugly ceiling because it was nothing she needed to care about. She wasn't responsible for calling a repair crew and painters. She'd thought it amusing that the lover could live under the mess.

She circled the room back to the desk and went through a second stack, this one all files. There were files with names. Sasha had never seen the lover's handwriting: the hard press of the pen, the careful, tight letters. The lover told her he worked as an indexer, and each file seemed connected to a book he might be working on. Rugs of the World. Jefferson. Italian Wines. Ella. That was her daughter's name. Ella. Inside the file were pages of notes, computer printouts of articles. "Acidification of Oceans." "Accessing Late-Triassic Extinctions."

There was a sheet torn from a loose-leaf, where he'd made a neatly numbered list, 1–20:

1. Take E. to the Smithsonian.

2. Take E. to zoo to show Armadillo and relationship to Ankylosaurus.

3. Talk to E. about Disaster Preparedness.

4. Talk to E. about Biological and Chemical Warfare.

5. Cybernetic Revolt.

6. Give list of current 168 extinctions.

7. Make THREE Survival Kits.

8. Take E. to the Big-Bone room @ MNH.

Sasha felt herself sway, and sank her knees to keep upright. Why had she ever spoken about Ella in this room? She stared down at her polished toes for balance. She'd told him about Ella's wobbly tooth. About the stuffed puppy and the pink rubbing blanket Ella hid when friends came to the house. She'd told him more about her daughter than she had about herself. Now she was standing without clothes on in his room. Now Sasha was naked in a room where her body did not belong.

Heat coughed from the pipes. The room was broiling. What instinct gone kerflooey would put so much at risk? He was making survival kits, three of them. "Come with me, my love," he'd said. She was wrong; she hadn't stepped into unexpected weather. She was her own catastrophe. Her own bolide collision. No, there were catastrophes much larger—unseen shifts to the system—she hadn't considered. Extinction. The underlying cause, the failure to adapt to changing conditions.

Had to go, something came up. Simple. Nothing too alarming. She left the note on a pillow.

❧

Sasha slid the mixing bowl over to her daughter. Ella knelt on a stool and propped against the counter, the whisk snicking against the bowl's metal sides. Ella poked the whisk into the center of each egg, making trails with the bright yokes.

"Some dinosaurs even ate the eggs of other dinosaurs," Ella announced. Sasha poured milk into a measuring cup, then steadied the bowl as Ella practiced the mixing strokes.

"Every species has predators," Ella spoke, using her meticulous science voice. "But are we predators?" Ella stopped whisking. "Are you and me?"

Sasha took a caught breath.

She saw how every answer might tilt unfavorably, a dissonant chorus of agendas belting out their positions. How she might tilt the answer in favor of her choice.

"We eat animals, sweetie. Some people would say we are." Sasha ran her hand down the smooth plank of her daughter's back.

Ella looked into the bowl with its foamy eggs. It seemed she might cry; her eyes had that same fullness when she came to apologize for bad behavior or unkind words. Sasha wanted to pour the milk quickly, unegg the eggs.

"If we didn't eat these, would they become chickens?" Ella said.

Sasha was relieved to say, "Nope, they're not fertile eggs."

"Who's the predator of our eggs?"

"Our eggs grow inside. We produce fewer, but they're safer than species that lay eggs." Sasha shaped her voice, stanced it with scientific authority. Limit the answers to satisfy the specific question. Ella knew about babies. Bring her to what already made sense. "Humans carry babies inside. That protects us. Make sense?"

Ella winced. "Mom, you don't actually think we're safe." Ella looked ready to ask all the questions. Like why Sasha hadn't been on time for pick-up and Ella had been the last waiting with the teacher. And why they were baking a celebration cake on a regular day when it was nobody's birthday. Why Sasha had rushed to take a shower before cooking rather than after cooking.

"Tell the truth." Ella was clearly trying to keep her voice steady, wanting to sound like she'd known everything all along. The I-know-more-than-you-think-I-do voice.

Sasha fought the urge to turn out an easy punch line. She could try to redirect Ella and say, We'll feel safer once this chocolate cake comes out of the oven.

"It's my job to keep you safe, sweetpea," she said quietly.

Ella insisted, "Tell me the truth."

Sasha thought of what Richard had said when she'd woken from her recurring dream that the house had burnt down. His hand pressed to her forehead, he'd said, "Look, we always manage. I'll keep us safe." Pulling her in close, his body shuddered back into its sleep. And Sasha, snugged next to him, tried to breathe in his rhythm. What had they managed, she wanted to wake him and ask. Such a delicate creature, a marriage. Hard enough to bungle through a day spent listening to the exaltations and treasons of one's own mothy heart. It should have made her generous. Instead, it made her preemptive.

A good man. Too good. He'd only ever been steady and true. Yet in the dark of their bedroom, she conjured not only Richard in other rooms with other bodies at odd times of day, but all his possible errors: tiny miscalculations leading to accruals of gross debt and ruin. An evolution of compounding errors right up to his inevitable confession, apology, and need for her forgiveness. She'd rather be in the wrong. She'd rather undo everything good first than imagine surviving Richard's mistakes.

"Well, are we?" Ella pulled up on her knees, shoulders winged back.

"We do our best." *Our best?*—a bald lie or the best kind of truth?

We hold hands crossing the street. Wear our bike helmets, seatbelts. Avoid the rip tide, shutter up and evacuate in hurricane weather. Draw charts, graphs, and erect whole meteorological stations to keep a measure of all inclement or advancing forces. Still we fuck up. In full sight of the right choice, we fuck up. And usually the important stuff.

And not for lack of knowing.

Sasha motioned for her daughter to stir while she poured milk, then sugar. The sugar made a thick ribbon and Ella cut the whisk through it, pulling it in swirls.

When Sasha had wakened, the dream flames insistent and pulsing, and Richard whispered, "Don't you trust I do my best to keep us safe?" Sasha never admitted that it was she who held the burnt match.

Ella scooched her chair to the stove, stirred chocolate squares and butter on the double boiler.

"Careful," Sasha said.

"I have this under control." Ella glared with Julia Child–level indignation.

Sasha's floured palms opened in mock contrition. "Hey, just trying to keep you safe," and the two of them laughed.

Wasn't this better than dinosaurs? she was tempted to ask her daughter. The dinosaurs came and went. No definitive reason, finally, for their demise. Wasn't it better to measure and pour, make sweets in a warm kitchen instead of worrying about birds with teeth? Better even, really, than unfaithful Louis Leakey. Instead of hands dusty from the excavation of early Hominoids, wasn't it better in a rigged-out kitchen, the early evening light sparkling the flour dust on their hands and hair?

When the front door closed, Sasha saw her daughter work to keep focus. Ella wanted to be found by her father, engaged in a serious baking project. She pressed the smiley face of M&M's into the chocolate frosting of their cake.

Sasha waited for the rattle of the closet hangers. She held breath for shoes dropped in their usual one clunk at a time, the weighted sound of his leather case, some clear, reliable sound that the person who had entered the house was her husband. But it was quiet. It was as if whoever was out there was waiting too. And everything was possible in those quiet moments, even whatever the worst of it might be, which Sasha knew was idiotic television drama, doomsday horror, but also good old logic, an entirely logically possible result—one of several—if the data of her day, her last two months was reliably charted. No, this was more than logic; something was deserved.

Ella looked so serious, intent on matters right before her. She pushed a red M&M and then another into the cake. Sasha scanned the kitchen for what she might use. The room was a big mess. It looked like the disaster had already struck. Cups and spoons and spatulas, bags of sugar and flour, the brown-glass vanilla bottle with a sticky dribble gummed beneath it. And chocolate everywhere. Not just chocolate in mixing bowls and pots, but chocolate on the stove and chocolate smears on the fridge and, somehow, chocolate streaked on the cabinet. There had been no proper cleanup as they'd gone along. Sasha lifted a paring knife from the cutting board.

"Fee Fi Fo Fum! Where are my women?" And there it was, of course, Richard's clear, open voice. And the thick sound of his socked feet skate-sliding on wood floors.

"Daddy," Ella shouted, "Daddy, you won't believe this."

"Whoohoo!" Richard said as he turned into the kitchen. "Is there anything better than coming home and seeing the two most beautiful women in the same kitchen?"

He stood behind his daughter, tipped her face back to him, kissed her forehead, then licked a print of chocolate off her nose.

Ella said in her best professional voice, "There's a little more I must do."

Sasha watched Richard turn slowly to find her. "Bit of a disaster," she said. She needed to adjust her face. But adjust to what?

"A fine disaster it is." Richard took up her hand and slipped the paring knife out of her hold.

"Just know you've got the best catastrophe cleanup service in the business," he said and began munching at Sasha's fingers, making loud lip-smacking sounds that started their daughter laughing.

Sasha looked at Richard's head curled over their daughter's hand. His hair was thick and dark, the same as Ella's. Sasha could practically parse Ella—Richard's hair, his eyes, Sasha's nose and chin. Ella seemed to have what was right and best of each of them.

But right was less the point than this, Ella wedging her way in between them, her parents adjusting to fit her, the M&M happy-face cake with its unfinished, crooked smile on the counter.

"We're getting Daddy covered in flour," Sasha whispered down to her daughter. "He's a mess."

"That's good. Then he'll be one of us," Ella said, marking an X on her father's woolen trouser leg with dirty, sugared hands.

THE HORN

She was the handsome boy sent out by Highdaddy as a handsome girl, not so wise as just lucky to remember how good a bowl of dirty water tasted.

She was the black-haired girl sent out to see what she could see.

She saw it like the girl he had taught, a girl quick to cut off her black curls and let the birds make nest with them, a girl to take trade with a sailor: his sloppy kisses for a belt, another's rough palm for a cap, a hand, a hand, a shove and grunt, until she had herself done up as a boy ready to step off the infested land.

She was ready to take her berth among men. They had exhausted themselves with the possibilities of her tiny feet and her tiny tongue and the skin of her tiny buttocks.

The mess kit was heavy; ash wood and boiled chunks made it wobble. She carried it high so as not to let it drop. The kit covered her eyes.

She was not only a boy, but the youngest here aboard, so the one to carry down, from the first noon on, the wooden midday kit, piled thick with boiled salt beef. Three days soaked in that harness cask and still the men called it salt horse. They called her Lucky, as they had called the one before her, a scrappy Indian of Russian persuasion who disappeared on the lee side of the Horn. They called it the Horn like it was a pronged bone at the end of the world.

It was Highdaddy's lesson, the lesson to hold her tongue, the girl's everyday quiet, that worked so well for her as a boy named Lucky.

She chewed well her portion of salted meat. When the smell grew foul, she had only to think of Highdaddy and she swallowed down the foul, chewed bits.

She stood up, this lucky boy, gave a full-table wink, gave it long and good and quiet. Just like Highdaddy had taught the girl to do.

She leaned the side of the wood tray against a wood shelf. She looked about Highdaddy's chamber. She looked for a proper table to lay out his meal.

The desk was red, the color of day-old blood.

She moved toward him, carrying the tray up, high and out. She set it on his desk, clearing the space for the bowls of Highdaddy and the polished silver fork and spoon and knife.

"Have you ears?" he asked. She could hear the edges of his voice and knew where she could go if she had to soothe or strip him.

The butt of his hand jammed against her throat. The ribbon pipe of her throat closed.

He let go.

She was there at the foremast and clewing the sails to the middle of the yard. She was in the galley with the cook, who sat, sooty among his steaming coppers. She was there checking the spare boats held in the bearers above the galley.

She was carrying the tray down to Highdaddy's chamber.

Even dead, the fish on the deck were handsome. Each morning, she kept two aside. She took one and threw it back to the sea. The other, with its faint flipping, she pocketed in her trousers. At night, just before going down to sleep, she fished out the fish from her pocket. Dried out, it had lost none of its silver sheen. She dropped it on the deck.

Highdaddy once made her show him her tongue.

"I thought so," he said.

He pinched her tongue between his fingers. The fingers slid down her tongue until they popped off. He pinched it harder this time so that when his fingers popped off she could see his fingertips were wet. She closed her mouth.

"Sit down," he said. "Sit down."

"They call you Lucky," Highdaddy said, cutting his food into smaller and smaller chunks. "Perhaps," he said, "it will do."

TRUST ME

"The job's the job. That's it," the woman explained. He doesn't want improvisation, no fancy suggestions, no extra stories, nothing personal—"He really, really, really dislikes personal," the woman said. Jaye looked at the woman's pinched face as she made a big to-do over each *really.* "There's no leeway. Strictly stay with what he asks for." Which in Jaye's case was taking over from where the woman had stopped reading Vasari's *The Lives of the Artists.*

Here, at Joe's, the last coffee place open after the summer season, Jaye learned the woman, Trish, was leaving Provincetown after three years, going down to Brooklyn to be a studio instructor at Pratt.

"You're a painter, too?" Trish asked as if this was a life problem, like heavy drinking or psoriasis.

"I know you'd think, given who he was, I mean who he is still, he'd maybe be interested—like in your work, or the current scene, what you were hoping for in the big bad art world. But he's not. Don't think I didn't try and don't think I've landed this gig in the city because of any connection to Maurice."

Jaye heard the intimacy of that name, Maurice, watched Trish's narrow laugh and felt already that Jaye wasn't getting a job so much as getting stuck with Maurice.

But Jaye thought it would be good to read Vasari's *The Lives of the Artists*. Even downright fortuitous, given her decision to quit her job and come to the Cape explicitly to study early and lost techniques. She knew of the book, mostly from a professor who'd quoted it and handed out the chapter on Giotto. She'd found that section kind of dull.

But even if Trish was laughing, it seemed like a good job, really, come on, reading for two hours each afternoon a book she'd always thought she should have read. And reading it to Maurice Stroud, a painter whose work Jaye had worshipped since she'd seen the first slide of it in art school. How bad could that be? And seventy-five an hour, cash, to read? How bad could that be? Besides, after spending five minutes with this Trish woman, Jaye knew she wouldn't want to hear Trish's personal tales, her woes, her loves or her art. If Jaye were being read to, she'd make rules too to keep Trish from straying from the text.

"Well, thanks," Jaye said. "I could use the job even if I thought holing up here off-season meant I'd manage without."

Trish pushed a single key across the counter at Jaye. "He'll want you to just come right in. I'll tell him it's set and that you'll be in tomorrow. It's all pretty straightforward. You're afternoon. There's a morning person for newspapers and magazines. Don't try to tidy up or touch stuff. There's person for everything. And even if you don't think it's possible, the blindness is complete."

Jaye nodded behind her coffee cup. Trish stood and buttoned her wool peacoat.

"And don't ask questions." Trish looked hard at Jaye. "You're cute and young but if you think he's butterupable, or that you can flatter him into talking about his big life, forget it."

Jaye's rental studio was large, with large north windows facing a garden the guy below her worked in all hours of the day. When Jaye took breaks, she'd see him with his brushy mane, bent over raised beds, even in October, when Jaye thought just about everything was done for. The guy was Sandy, a name so ridiculously beachy that Jaye assumed it was a nickname.

"We'll have lettuces for a while," Sandy said, handing Jaye a baggie of leaves. He'd knocked on her door though it was open with the screen door unlatched, and then, before she could stand from her table, he'd walked into her studio with the easy air of someone who'd been in and out of the room for years. "You'd be surprised how long I'll feed us out of this yard."

It took Jaye a beat to realize he was including her. She was used to feeding herself, grazing mostly, nuts, a yogurt, tea all day. She counted vitamins as food.

"This is the barest the studio's ever been. The last guy was a total hoarder, like almost the certifiably sick kind of deranged thing, banging shit up the stairs night and day. You sure you're a painter? I've seen this studio through a lot of years, a lot of artists, and even the neat ones are slobs."

Jaye looked around—neatly made bed in the corner, simple worktables practically empty, blank walls. Even painted over, the walls showed marks where others had hung canvasses.

"I'm starting way, way back." Jaye wondered why she owed this guy any explanation. "Silverpoint drawing, later I'll grind my pigments." She showed the finely sanded gessoed boards she'd prepared, the silver point, like lead, fixed in the holder.

"That's so way cool," Sandy said. "Way cool." And despite how goofy he sounded, how all his enthusiasm rattled Jaye, she found herself showing him how with silver you built up the darks with the steady light marks.

She was early, though she'd tried her best not to be early. It was only a few minutes but she thought of Trish's warnings and decided against anything that Maurice Stroud might consider improvising, taking leeway.

Jaye hoped she'd hear something inside but the door was shut.

"Hi, I'm Jaye," Jaye said, coming into the room just when her watch said 4 p.m. He was sitting in a wingback chair. He didn't nod or speak and it made her feel that she'd already made a mistake. But fuck it—she wasn't supposed to even have manners and say her name?—and so she stood close to him, saying it again, "I'm Jaye," and held out her hand.

"Hello, Jaye," he said formally. He didn't say his name. It occurred to Jaye that he didn't know her hand was outstretched. He looked like the photographs she'd seen of him, the notable shock of white hair, the high brow and angular face. The great lean frame, his long legs crossed. Jaye remembered a magazine photograph of him in this same position outdoors, at a party or maybe the racetrack, surrounded by women, including his last wife and a woman who it was known had been a longtime lover. He didn't look much older than the last published pictures, which Jaye figured must have been twenty or thirty years old by now. It was amazing how long he'd looked like this, like a handsome old man. Seeing him, she realized she'd expected decrepitude. Old and blind, living all year in a small apartment that was once his summer studio in a mostly closed-up summer town, this was the pathetic pictured she'd concocted of the great painter.

"Have a seat, Jaye," he said, and she realized that she'd been standing right in front of him. "You'll find the bookmark."

Jaye sat in a facing wingback and picked up the book. It was the first volume, a Penguin Classic, clearly read many times. She let it fall open to the pencil that served as the bookmark.

"I'm excited about reading Vasari," she said. "I've read parts before but never the entire work." It was out of her mouth before she'd realized she'd said it and she looked over, expecting a frown or even some sort of rebuke. He was sitting in his chair quietly waiting, his face slanted in anticipation of her beginning to read.

She liked reading aloud. She had a knack for it; since she'd been a child, she'd looked forward to any opportunity to read, raising her hand in class to read a Gwendolyn Brooks poem or keeping car rides bearable on family vacations by reading whole novels aloud over the two days it took them to reach the family cottage in Nova Scotia. In graduate school she'd incorporated into her final painting project a spoken text that came through hidden mikes.

But now Jaye felt herself straining to deliver and her pronunciation, her sentence rhythm seemed stilted. She'd begun where the page marker had been left, at the "Life of Paolo Uccello." She tripped over easy words—*foreshortened, tempera, pergola.* She looked up and Maurice was sitting in his chair, his head resting against the high back.

His eyes were closed, or partly closed, maybe just the eyelids relaxed, like blinds half drawn. Jaye had never been in a room with a blind person—unless you counted the Stevie Wonder concert she'd gone to in Chicago. She hadn't thought about what it would be like, reading to a blind man, but, now that she was here, she realized she didn't know the rules.

Didn't blind people have super-developed other senses?

Maybe Maurice could hear her staring at him. She wished she'd showered before coming over. When his hand moved close to his mug, his fingers moving slowly on the table, Jaye felt herself pause in her reading. Should she read right through? Should she give him the chance to locate what he needed?

Vasari was pretty critical of Uccello, Jaye thought, claiming he was too focused on perspective and not focused enough on the figure. Vasari was so tough—finally, in the final sentence, calling the work *rewarding to those who have used it since.* Of course she'd known Uccello's name but she couldn't really think of his work. And why should a fascination with perspective over the figure necessarily plunk him on the second tier? She wished the book had plates—so she could connect what she'd read with a painting. Vasari at least credited Uccello's mastery of animals. The horses, the lions—she thought maybe she would recognize a painting but animals might be any of those guys. She wanted to ask Maurice what he thought, if he trusted Vasari's judgment.

"That's good," Maurice said, when she got to end of the chapter.

"Should I keep reading?" Jaye said, hearing a formal quality in her voice. It was weird to be in a room with a man who hadn't seen her, didn't know what she looked like. It made her tentative. She felt only partly there. At least she hadn't slipped into shouting or whispering to compensate.

"The next is Ghiberti, Lorenzo Ghiberti. Or maybe you want to talk about Uccello? I've got to admit I knew his name, of course, but not much else."

Maurice turned his face to Jaye. He seemed to be looking at her.

Appraising her. It was weirding Jaye out. Not just the looking at her or through her but that he kept staring like he was really looking the way he might if he were drawing her, even though she knew—in fact kept saying in her head—he's blind he's blind he's blind.

"I'd like you to read it over," Maurice said, settling back, resuming his position, with his head leaning against the wing of his chair, his face turned and his eyes shuttered down.

"From the start?" Jaye asked. She'd never done that. Who did that?

Maurice didn't say anything and so Jaye read the chapter on Uccello all over again.

"Inspired rapture." Jaye was picking at the last in the wooden salad bowl. "Vasari would call this inspired rapture."

Sandy smiled over at her and Jaye saw he had a clip of dark lettuce wrapped around a tooth.

She'd taken to going downstairs and having dinner with Sandy. The salads were unlike anything Jaye had eaten, which seemed improbable—since wasn't lettuce just lettuce? But the platters Sandy whipped up had greens that were bitter and nutty, cooked beet greens mixed in and other stuff—shaved root-looking things Jaye couldn't identify—

and dressings that were gingered and flecked with dill. It amazed her how tenderly Sandy spoke about his garden, like every fucking bumpy potato was a special treat from nature that Sandy was lucky enough to coax into the world.

"Inspired? He's a colossal asshole. Who needs all that judgment?" Sandy said. "I am so not into my efforts being evaluated by some Vasari."

So not into—it made Jaye feel like a schmuck that she picked on the way Sandy spoke. Especially when he was feeding her every night. Feeding her and providing her with the only conversation available between time in the studio and reading to Maurice. Reading to Maurice, she might as well be alone. Pretty much the same every afternoon. She knew to read each chapter twice. Then he'd make his way to the bathroom. She'd get herself a glass of water and she'd put a second down on the table by Maurice's chair. Jaye was eager to poke around, look at all the paintings clustered on the walls but she didn't want to be caught roaming around the room when he came from the bathroom. He scared her.

Jaye liked going over what she'd read at dinner, talking about what she could recall after two readings. How much Sandy understood was up for grabs, but Sandy smiled and let her talk. And looked at her.

After two hours with Maurice, that was reassuring. Yesterday and today she wore lipstick over to Maurice's and a tank top with a low neckline. Tonight she'd kept them on for dinner. Maybe Sandy didn't understand one thing about perspective or the figures of Masaccio. Maybe Sandy was just being polite when she talked about Ghiberti's bronze doors. When there was a break in the conversation, Sandy told her about his Jade Cross cabbages.

Sandy described what he'd rigged up for the gardens in case of an early frost. Plastic jugs cut to fit over the broccoli, and long tarps and even some sheets and towels to lie over the beds of cabbage and kale. He was prepared.

"But we're still in T-shirts," Jaye said.

"Please, don't I know it." Sandy grinned at her skimpy tank top.

Jaye imagined Maurice would be impressed by her exploration of silverpoint. It was an odd coincidence, her having taken up a Renaissance drawing technique that had all but disappeared, just as she'd taken a job reading *The Lives of the Artists*. Maybe Maurice didn't even know about silverpoint. Why would he? His own work was bold strokes—defiant, large brushwork, mostly black and white. But he'd have questions. She'd describe how silverpoint work was even slower than she'd imagined it would be. It took such patience. No chance for a quick impressive mark. Tones were to be built slowly, with little chance for contrast. It was all about subtlety.

Given his paintings, why Maurice was interested in *The Lives* was a question Jaye couldn't answer. She wanted to talk about his generation—de Kooning, Rauschenberg, Motherwell, all his pals. She'd read about their all-night, drunken discussions. In addition to his wives, Maurice had been linked to a sculptor named Olga for some years, a poet, Myra, and others whose names Jaye didn't know.

But there was no talking, never, not a simple question about her life outside his studio. As far as Jaye knew, he didn't even know she was a painter. There was never any reflection on what they read each afternoon. Only a "Hi, Jaye" when she first walked in and "that's enough today" if he wanted her to stop before the two hours were up.

Sandy was at the stove, narrating the meal he was making. Kale, garlic and pine nuts in an oiled wok. A chicken garnished with rosemary branches just out from the oven. Potatoes roasted with onion and cilantro.

"I went to Maurice's in my slip today," Jaye said. She sat on Sandy's futon couch, balancing an appetizer plate of curried cashew paste and carrots on her jeans. "I mean only wearing a slip."

"Dude, you are totally off on your dressing choices for your various engagements of the day," Sandy said. "Except, of course, as a gardener, I have an awesome imagination for what's below the surface."

"I wanted to see if there was any reaction."

"Don't tell me. Turns out the old fucker's not even blind."

"Nothing, at first nothing. Or that's what I thought. Until I saw his head shift—the slightest shifting, almost like a twitch—when I moved. Then I realized he could hear the slip."

"And?"

"I felt like an idiot, like I'd shown up for school in pajamas or naked."

"Anything happen?"

"I just read the section on Raphael and tried not to cross or uncross my legs."

Sandy cut the roasted chicken, arranging the pieces on a platter. He brandished a leg on the fork. "I'm betting Maurice begs for Raphael again tomorrow."

Jaye loved the way the silverpoint emerged, the buildup of crosshatched lines, but it was slow going, bent over the tablework, and in the end the subtlety, day after day, was frustrating. She had to be so careful. No room for mistake, the palest mark showed. And pressing too hard could crack the gessoed surface. She had to work in bursts. Silverpoint, more than working in pencil, demanded that she render shape or else the surface became spidery. She'd spent the morning on a girl's face. The girl was curious, as if she were hearing something close by, a bird. The girl tilted her head to locate what tree it sang from.

Now, here in the pasta and canned-goods aisle, Maurice was pushing a cart. A dark-haired, butchy-built woman held his arm, talking quietly to him. Jaye had seen her around, driving a pickup, drinking coffee at Joe's, playing pool in one of the year-round bars, licking salt off a woman's fist before doing a shot. She and Maurice looked comfortable together, so comfortable that Jaye wondered if she was Maurice's daughter. There were others who came to the apartment, a young metal-sculptor, who made coffee and read the newspaper each morning, an older Portuguese woman who cleaned the studio once a week. There were others, but Jaye assumed they were all like herself, hardly there at all except for their specific tasks.

Maurice was laughing. He had a wide-open laugh. Outside his studio, Maurice looked taller. Jaye was struck by how really handsome he was, robust, distinguished, thick, long white hair. He seemed to Jaye like the aloof visiting artist who shows up at an art school and soon is nose to nose in conversation with the leggy painter who quits school to be his studio assistant.

"Fusilli," Maurice said.

"With the peas and bacon, that'll be perfect." The woman squeezed close on his arm.

Jaye lingered in front of the canned tomatoes as Maurice and the woman pushed up the aisle. Maurice leaned a little on the cart but he seemed sure-footed, like he knew his way around. He wouldn't even know Jaye was there; she could turn and leave. Or she could say hello. She would. She should. Just a basic "Hi there, Maurice," all casual, like she and Maurice ran into each other in town all the time.

"Hey, Maurice, looky here. Jaye's here," the woman said.

They were practically cart to cart. Jaye grabbed a can of plum tomatoes off a shelf.

"You know, Jaye, who's your new Trish." The woman laughed and then, looking at Jaye, winked. "The new and *way improved* Trish."

"I'll be seeing you soon, won't I, Jaye?" Maurice's whole manner was jaunty. "We're at Piero della Francesca. Always interesting. And good to see you like pasta too."

❧

"Come on, *good to see*—it's an expression," Sandy said. He was picking lettuces, placing them on a cloth towel like they were something expensive and breakable. "It's not something you chuck from your vocabulary just 'cause suddenly you actually can't see. You see what I'm saying," Sandy laughed.

"No. But why was he suddenly all Mr. Chatty?"

"Hang on," Sandy said, springing up. Everything about Sandy was loose and limby: his hair shaggy, what rolled off his tongue doing so in its own shaggy way. Jaye found herself wanting to reach out to touch the gold in his hair. "Before you go over, I've got something else for Maurice."

Jaye waited in the garden, where she'd never been without Sandy. It was clear she'd never really taken much notice of it. But now it seemed obvious that the garden would be her next silverpoint—the long, full brussels-sprout wands, beds of tight, curly lettuces, the wide-ribbed pumpkin and squashes. She walked around, squinting to take the garden down to forms and lines. The geometry of the raised beds. Maybe she'd even draw it from above, from her studio window. Vasari was always commenting on an artist's attentions to mathematics.

When Sandy came out, she was standing on a chair, looking

down at the broccoli.

"Don't jump!" Sandy shouted, "Life's worth living!" and in a quick motion, he swept her off the chair.

"Is there time before the frost?" Jaye didn't want to lose her chance. "I'll help you cover the garden at night."

"Whoa, little missy, that's quite an offer for a farm boy."

Sandy slid her down slowly and Jaye squirmed to back away from him. Of course, shaggy-dude, thirty-year-old Sandy was another one of the eternal boys. There was a whole club of them. She'd met her share in art school.

"Give this to Maurice, from me, okay?" Sandy looked at the little Ziploc bag. Fresh, tight buds of weed. "From my secret garden." Sandy bowed as if by way of explanation.

"For Maurice?" Of course they knew one another, Sandy and Maurice; they'd both been year-rounders for years, of course they did. "You give Maurice weed?"

"It's a small-ass town, Jaye, and a long-ass winter. Best we can, we all help each other through it."

"Can I look at the work on the walls?" Jaye asked, but without waiting for permission, she got up and began to circle the room. She'd put the weed in the noisy icebox and gotten ready with the Vasari. She felt Maurice tracking her and, sure enough, when she pivoted from the small collection of Philip Guston ink pieces, Maurice was turned, his long body twisted in the chair, doing whatever the staring thing was that he did.

"These are amazing," Jaye said.

"They're Christmas cards," Maurice said, as if Jaye were some kind of idiot and couldn't read the "Merry Christmas" scrawled on each card.

The work on the walls was a jumble of pieces—artists Jaye had never heard of right next to pieces by pretty much every major American artist of the the post–Second World War era. It was a who's who; the walls were jig-saw-puzzle covered with crappy frames, old mats. A curator would have conniption. A lot of it was personal, notes scrawled on the bottom of a line drawing, birthday wishes and inscrutable messages.

Jaye identified Maurice's work mixed among the patchwork of paintings, mostly small pieces, studies for larger work; there was one small gouache on board that Jaye thought she'd seen the large version of in the Modern. But none of the grand pieces he was best known for, the huge canvasses with their rugged, almost aggressive brushwork, were hanging. Jaye took her time, enjoying breaking Maurice's rules, lingering over a picture, saying whatever came to her—the oohs and ahs and that's amazings!—but also "I mean a valentine from Louise Nevelson, that's crazy. Was she ever your lover?"

"Can we please get on with Vasari?" Maurice's voice was subdued, exhausted, as if he'd returned from a long distance.

Jaye came back to her chair opposite him and picked up the book. She felt triumphant. What was she trying to win? She wanted him to notice that it wasn't just a Nevelson that she could recognize, it was the more obscure painters—she'd commented on the Philip Pavia marble piece, and a landscape by Edwin Dickinson. She could hold her own in a conversation. Everyone else in town seemed perfectly chummy with Maurice. Sandy fucking gave Maurice gifts of pot, probably came over and split a doobie. And there was the pickup-truck dyke cracking up with Maurice while they wheeled around the supermarket. Jaye didn't want to be *the new Trish*. Who'd want to talk to Trish? Jaye was a painter. She wanted real conversation.

"I'm looking forward to reading about Piero della Francesca," Jaye said, knowing the reading would start only when she started. "I've been studying early pigments for a while. It's the next place I'm going after silverpoint. Anyway, in his *Madonna del Parto* her whole dress is a made from lapis lazuli from Afghanistan. It was very costly. Very beautiful."

Maurice nodded and Jaye took that as a good sign. She gave him a chance to respond but he didn't. She didn't fucking need to be treated like shit by an old, stoned, blind man. This, she decided, would be her last day.

But when, in the middle of the first paragraph, Jaye read that Piero della Francesca was *regarded as a great master of the problems of regular bodies, both arithmetical and geometrical, but . . . was prevented by the blindness that overtook him in his old age, and then by death,* Jaye choked up. She tried to keep on reading, getting to the end of the sentence but she couldn't.

"I'm sorry," she tried to say, but she'd begun crying so hard she couldn't get out more than a few stuttery sounds. When Jaye could manage—and it took a while—taking short gulping breaths, that set her off again. And then when it was quiet enough for her to get out more than sobs, she closed her eyes and said, "I'm an idiot, a complete fucking idiot."

It was silent in the room and Jaye squinted open her eyes, blinking to clear off the tears.

Maurice was smiling, nothing mean in his smile, no pity, no condescension, just a good, open, handsome smile. "I've seen worse," he said and then he winked at her.

Not the whole tree or even any of the tree's trunk, but a couple of limbs had emerged in the silverpoint, a branch dense with foliage above the girl's head. The leaf work was pleasing to Jaye. She felt she was duplicating the growing process, starting with a small curling shape and working the lines as veins in the leaves. It was great mat of leafage. She had a book of Dürer's open on her table, mostly woodcuts but also a silverpoint, an early self-portrait, on which he had written, *When I was a child.* Dürer in his travels might have met some of the Italians in Vasari's *Lives.* Dürer's woodcut trees were like terrible bodies, twisted and uncomfortable, ready to crawl or tangle. Jaye wanted her silverpoint forest to be gentle, like a bower, enveloping, each leaf glittering in late afternoon light. She wanted the girl with her curious attention to be safe. The bird the girl could hear was there, a blue jay, the artist's self-portrait—just as the old masters included—hiding, mostly obscured by leaves. It delighted Jaye, the cleverness.

Jaye could hear Sandy whistling whole songs down in his garden. Every once in a while he gave a little whoop or she heard him talking to himself. Jaye wished she could be chirpy when she worked. Most days she couldn't even work to classical music. She thought about the light in his hair, the way his fingers nimbled around the plants. She thought about the way he'd lifted her off the chair and slid her down his body length.

"Not good, not good," whispered Jaye. It wasn't even daylight saving times and Jaye couldn't believe that she was here in her studio thinking about sleeping with a gardener who whistled the TV theme song from *Friends*.

"Hey hey, Jaye, want some?" It was Maurice's pickup-truck, grocery-store dyke, sitting on Sandy's kitchen counter, drinking red wine and pouring Jaye a big glass before she'd had a chance to answer. "I'm Beth," she said. "Sandy's too much a kid to ever actually carry out actual introductions."

Beth went back to telling Sandy about someone named Terese who'd come back from Oregon and taken an apartment above her old lover's apartment, where Terese could now hear her old lover having the same fight with his new lover that he's had with Terese. It seemed that Beth was also saying that she'd started sleeping with this Terese.

"Sandy, do you remember when Terese was always running over to hide in our place?" Beth said. "She's the other half of the reason we fell apart, Sandman. You just couldn't help yourself." Beth had a big laugh—affectionate and thick with private history.

"Well, Bethie, now it seems you can't help yourself. And that's fucking karma," Sandy said, throwing chillies and garlic like punctuation into the oiled wok.

Terese, Sandy, Beth, the old lover, the new lover—this town in winter was way, way, way too small. One winter or another, had everyone pretty much slept with everyone, been their dealer and then wound up with them in detox?

"Maurice adores you." Beth poured more wine into Jaye's mostly full glass.

"Adores me?" Jaye snapped, "What could Maurice possibly adore? I read. I give him a glass of water. I don't speak. I leave." She left out, And sometimes I fall apart like a blubbering nutcase.

"He says he loves the intelligence of your voice. And, baby, anyone who shows up in a torn, pink slip is going to attract Maurice's attention."

"Thanks, Sandy." Jaye was glad for an absolute, complete, foolproof forever reason to never again for one second consider sleeping with him. "For the record, it wasn't pink or torn."

Beth was laughing her big, raucous laugh. "Oh no, Jaye, the source was the master himself. The guy is all ears. Well, and hands when he gets lucky." Jaye watched the wine slosh dangerously in Beth's glass as Beth cracked up. "I guess the torn pink was a wishful addition from Maurice's imagination."

Later, after dinner, after Beth had gone to meet up with Terese, Sandy and Jaye blanketed lettuces and hatted broccoli with the cut jugs and unrolled plastic sheeting over the kale and cabbage.

"This actually works?" The garden looked all wrong, dramatically wrong, like a crime scene. The lumpy forms pressed under the plastic, the odd milky color of the sheeting as it caught the outdoor floodlights. Sandy clipped the plastic to the wood of the raised beds.

"You sure about this frost?" Jaye considered that better than drawing the open garden would be drawing these strange, draped shapes. The plastic jugs like headstones. The garden as a morgue.

"I'm not sure about anything. Just always cautious."

"But what if it doesn't work?"

"I'll harvest what I can, then start planning for our spring." Sandy looked at Jaye.

There it was again, that hopeful feeling, knotting up in Jaye's chest.

"Thanks for helping, Jay-bird."

"Jay-bird?"

Sandy did a little shruggy thing with his shoulders, smiled his crooked boyish smile. Jay-bird, Sandman, Bethie—everything was a nickname around here—it was all too much for Jaye. Let alone "Jay-bird" when the blue jay had become her signature.

"Can't help it, Jay-bird," Sandy said, coming up close and slipping his hands into the back pockets of Jaye's jeans. "All that wanna-fly wanna-stay motion in you—I'm digging it big time."

Jaye announced that she needed to talk about Botticelli.

"Do we have to?" Maurice asked after her second reading. But he didn't say no and Jaye took the question as a yes.

Sure, Vasari said of one painting that it showed Botticelli's complete mastery of craft. But Vasari's Botticelli didn't seem to be the profoundly important painter history claimed. Vasari spent most of the chapter showing what a prodigal spendthrift the guy was. A joker, a good teacher, but, in the end, Vasari claimed, Botticelli was an old, useless man on crutches, unable to even stand upright. Why not read about Botticelli from someone who has greater historical perspective?

"That's what I love," said Maurice, his head tilting as if talking to someone just out of reach. "It's not exactly *People Magazine* but it's all quite local. Who was famous? Who was jealous? Who was destitute?

Fame created and talent squandered."

"But *The Primavera* or *The Birth of Venus* are like minor mentions for Vasari." Jaye heard the *like* in her sentence and wanted to do it over. "The substance seems thin in so much of Vasari; you'd never know what was going to matter in history."

"That's what I love." Maurice was moving his head in almost-clichéd blind Stevie Wonder style, that big, ecstatic, Stevie smile transposed on Maurice's face. "That, my gem of a reader, is just exactly what this old man loves."

"You read over and over, you read this book like a religious text every day because it hardly matters?" Jaye felt heavy in her head.

"No, no, no." Maurice's eyes had closed and somehow that made Jaye feel better. "I'm interested that Vasari took it upon himself to chronicle his time. Vasari is talking into history. He's talking past the rulers and the forces of nature that left so much earlier work broken and anonymous. He's saying, 'This was us, so and so learned from so and so, and this guy was limited by vanity or illness or skill.'"

"You think I'm trying too hard?" Jaye thought of her strict plan for a year researching and making her way through the history of painting techniques.

Maurice's face turned to her but his eyes were still closed. "Appetite is a sign of health. Is there another way to try?"

"I don't know. You're the one who knows stuff. I'm really at the beginning of my career." But when Jaye said *career*, she remembered that Masaccio was twenty-six when he died. She remembered the praise Vasari heaped on him—for Masaccio's proportion and judgment. Vasari had called him a pioneer.

Then there was a long silence between them. Maurice's legs were stretched out, crossed at the ankles, the wale of his corduroy pants worn silky. Jaye looked at his long legs for a while, then at the afternoon light as it squared against a wall of his collected paintings. The light was moving, turning the corner in the room. The light had changed since Jaye began with Maurice. It was late fall and she could feel how little light each day held.

Jaye went to the wall and stood in front of a small drawing by Maurice. The darks were thick, almost impenetrable, and there was a world of dense hatching behind the lines that dominated the surface. It was a beautiful, small piece, a study, she suspected. Next to it was a drawing by Maurice's wife, a reclining nude, her head thrown back so that the focus was almost obscenely on the passage down her thighs to her pubis and her stomach. In the scrawl Jaye could make out *for you last night, promiscuously.*

Jaye walked over and kissed Maurice on his cheek. He took her hand as she started to step away.

"This is why I prefer reading without talking," Maurice said.

The silver on the gessoed boards had begun to change. It was softening, browning a bit, a luminosity that gave the girl's face a slightly ghostly tinge. Jaye had thought the color shift would take longer when she'd researched the technique. It felt a little like the piece was developing in a darkroom.

Looking at the board, Jaye decided the problem with silverpoint, or her problem with silverpoint, was that it looked more like illustration than art. She'd tried a Renaissance technique with Modern concerns. The setting of the trees was classical, almost a primeval forest, but the girl bore an almost pornographic countenance, as if she might be dragged out of the woods and into a TV music video. She wasn't Little Red Riding Hood innocent of the wolf's intentions. This silverpoint girl was never innocent; she was raised with a belly piercing and infomercials about Viagra. Still, for all of the slow work, the drawing looked cartoonish.

Sandy bounded into Jaye's studio early the next morning, announcing the first frost.

"I don't want to look," she said. "I'm asleep." She felt the chill even under her covers. It was still mostly dark in the room. Sandy knocked against the bed like a restless, loping dog.

"You've got to look now, Jay-bird. Trust me on this one."

"I don't trust you," she said, rolling close to the wall.

"Oh, Jay-bird, you do trust me but you just don't wanna trust a fool like me."

He scooped her up, covers and all, and walked with her across the studio to the window that looked over his garden. She kept her eyes closed, to resist his excitement. But she could feel how bright it was in the room, and when she opened her eyes, Sandy was standing with her before the large window. But that was all she could clearly identify.

Outside, the world was unlike anything she could recognize: shimmering rectangles, strange shapes pressing up from below, so much light, blue white—it must be moonlight—a bright sheet against the garden wall, and glimmering in the frost. This actually *was* the garden. The garden hose, a spiral of ice, looked otherworldly.

"I'm crazy for this!" she kicked her feet like a kid. When was the last time she'd done a thing like that? She kicked again, hugging tightly to Sandy, and he danced with her up in his arms, jigging up to and then backing away from the window.

"No, stay here," she insisted when they came close to the window again. She saw a series of large paintings, fantastic, strange, messy, done under the pressure of moonlight and weather. Immediate, intense. They would contain this joy.

"I need to see this every day."

"You can't see anything the same every day. So take a good long look, my little Jay-bird. Look and look and look because by tonight it's last summer's garden." Sandy knocked his head lightly against Jaye's head. "Today I'll harvest the whole shebang. Then for a few more nights we'll dine like kings. After that, every trace but what we are able to hold onto in our sorry, lonely cabezas is pretty much gone."

HE'S BACK

HE FOUND HER WITH THE BOY, THE TUB WATER BLUED AROUND THEM, so he knew just how long they had been there, soaping and soaping at each other, the boy wearing sudsy breasts and slipping over her arms, or sloped against her while she turned the frilled pages of some wet book. The boy, sculling and fluttering, finned against her and said, "He's back."

Not for long.

Not for long would he stand for it, the daily shed in that tub: hair and skin in pages, the boy's boats, all of her soaps, a creamy gray outline that lapped over them when they moved. And all that movement, her leg lifting from the water, the boy's dunking head, pointed toes, the watery swash of tits—not for long—not for long—or the way sometimes they pretended to have been asleep, and Did he have to be so noisy, she asked, winking up at him, that way he walked in whenever he came back?

He could be quiet.

Wasn't that the truth, walking in on them, midday in that tub, the boy looking up from where he knelt over her, his fingers doing a lacy thing on her throat.

No, they were not asleep. Not in the midday light or in the evenings when she posted candles about the room, so that he walked in to where they glowed up at him from the tub.

He would not have the chance to wake them. Not ever. That was also for certain truth. Look at the boy. He could barely lie still, let alone drift to sleep, fishing about with her in that water, flipping and flipping, casting his leg over her leg, smearing her clay masks in jagged lines over his cheek. They could barely get the boy to sleep at any hour, with the boy always calling for one more last waking thing.

Quiet, he could be quiet.

She had better, at the least, know that by now.

They did not even have to be in the water. It was everywhere. Water, water, overflowed, left murky in the tub, drips, towels dropped in hallways, a trek of powder footprints to where he found her with the boy, painting all those toenails some crazy shade of red.

"Look at my boy," he said, and they glanced up at him, the two of them looking as if they had never seen him before.

As if they had never seen him before!

What did they take him for?

Wherever they were, he knew, he just knew, they were lying in wait, the boy shouting before he had even gotten into the room, "You too! You too! Take off your shoes!"

He had done that and he would not do it again, letting them paint him red or suffering the lip outliner and clip-on earrings. What kind of clown did they take him for, smeary smile and rouged-up cheeks, just what did they take him for?

He would take them. What would they think of that, taking them out of those rooms and onto the street, where she would have to see how others went about with their boys—buttoned up, in coats, in hand?

Forget about her.

He would just take the boy, and to a dry place: sawdust on the floors, meat crisp on bones.

The boy said, "Yes, I'd like that."

The boy said he wanted it juicy, pink, cut off the bone, with a drink that bubbled. He ordered the boy a malted.

A frog's mouth, that's what the boy said the mother looked like when the hair parted.

Not to look. That is what he told the boy.

"At what?" she asked, coming in, stopping in front of an oval mirror to dot and blend something creamy and pink under her eyes.

He wanted to tell the boy how still worse was the gawk of those lips when the boy's own head had pushed out. Now, that was a sight not to be seen. And he had almost done it, squinting down to the blur so as to almost not see anything. But still, it was all too much seen, the stretched-open wreck of her, pulled to tearing, the way her face stretched out, too, all red and ugly with effort and, after all of it—bloody water, bloody shit, bloody head—after all was too much seen, the doctor waving him over, saying, "Oh, I know your type. So come on. Come right here. Get ready to catch it."

But he had seen it, the boy had. That was her doing; she was no doubt letting him look at the whole thing, holding nothing back from the boy, flaps and hood and clasp, no doubt going ahead and telling the boy what everything was called. Where else would the boy have learned? Not from him, God knows. God knows there was hardly a moment she would let him have alone with the boy, always her with some urgent need, calling the boy back to tuck a loose strand of hair behind his ear, having to give the boy one last before-bed special kiss, and then, no doubt, another three at least.

No, he had found her with the boy in the plain light of day, the boy bobbing about in her scented water and the boy announcing with not the least fear that she had a *giant*, and her laughing, winking up at him, saying, Wasn't the boy so smart about everything, learning everything faster than she could find what to teach him?

So smart?

He would show them smart.

He would teach them both a thing or two.

They were not anywhere.

There was water. Water everywhere, damn near a flood he had walked in on, coming home just in time, he thought, to save the goddamn house at least. A wreck, that's how it looked, everywhere water, and dirty damn water, too, the way she left all the rooms week by week to collect dust. Not a chance could he say anything about it, her throwing him such a look if he so much as mentioned cleaning.

"If you want a maid, get a maid," she said.

Thank God he had come when he had.

Just in time to save the filthy house from drowning.

What was she thinking? What was she possibly thinking? What could she be thinking going out like that? Not some few drips. Not some leaky faucet. Nothing less than a running tub. What was it with her? And couldn't he just see already how it would be, her coming home from who-knows-where, and without a word to say about anything? Hardly so much as a glance she'd have for him after all he had been through, buckets and buckets, wringing the mop not twenty, not one hundred times with her dust water, her dirt water, picking out bits of her hair, her strings and feathers—from what, feathers?—but, yes, picking feathers out from the mop.

And those towels. Impossibly heavy, those towels of hers, clumped all in a wet, dirty clump—he had a mind to throw them out once and for all, those towels, better than break his back, heaving and wringing. He was surprised at that: that she hadn't even the mind to think of those precious towels. God knows it seemed sometimes they were all she did have a mind about.

Certainly they were all she managed to clean, with her particular way of folding them, snatching his towel out from him before he was halfway dry and folding it in threes as if he didn't know by now that threes was the way she wanted it done. Her way, oh yes, that she could be bothered by. But shutting off the faucet? She could not be bothered by that, could she? And hot water at that. His ankles scalded in her water. Let the house drown, he thought. Might as well, for all she'd notice. She'd just be there with a stack of new towels, walking around a new set of rooms.

The boy was not any better. What could you expect? Spending his days with her and her soaps and her towels.

The boy probably thought it was just fine, fishing about like some swishy thing. But what did she think, that it was okay for a kid to spend his days puckered and gilled and bloated with water?

Or did she think at all? Certainly not, if this flooded-out house was any indication of her level of thought.

Thinking or not, she had better get ready.

He would tell her as soon as she walked in the door.

When was she walking in? Just where was she? Down to the store for new perfume or whatnot, certainly not for anything to eat. My God, she barely ate a thing if they couldn't eat it right in the tub with them. Soggy cardboard—he had picked up plenty of that in his day.

He was nobody's maid. Nobody's mop-it-up maid, he sure as hell wasn't. She had better know that by now. He would let her know that. He would let her have it as soon as she walked in. It would be soon, too. How could she survive out on those streets one minute, a regular fish out of water out there, her practically shredding her clothes before she had even gotten through the front door?

He would find the right kind of maid, all right.

Yes, he would.

He would find a sweet one. He would go out and find the boy a real sweet one. He would find one who scarcely needed all those lotions she was always smushing on herself. The boy would like that. He was no fool, that boy. He would see the difference soon enough. It might take a bit, time enough to dry out that waterlogged brain of his, but he would see the difference soon enough.

He would let that froggy see some real lips.

Oh yes, she would be back soon. With that boy of hers.

She came back wet.

The boy, too.

She came back wet, and without a towel or a lotion or any of the oily, sweet smells he thought she had gone out to get. She came back wet and late and the boy pressed wetly to her. She peeled the boy from her, laid him down in the tub and ran the water.

The boy slept.

She stripped out of her wet dress and underthings without so much as giving him a nod, not to mention a decent hello, not to mention the flimsy explanation he had expected from her, at the very least.

The boy stirred in the tub, lapping thinly from side to side like the too-thin twig of a child she had made of him. Anyone could see that, that the boy had barely anything to him. He was all stick. She had made sure of that, hadn't she—never taking the boy out to a park where he might run a bit with other boys. No, there was not even the name of a single boy that he could name. There was not one single boy for the boy. She had made sure of that, hadn't she, keeping the child home without even the pretext of his having a cold.

She ran it hot, the tub.

Without so much as a nod, she had come back.

Wasn't it he that had come back just in time?

Wasn't it his evening that had passed, mopping up her mess? Wasn't he the one who had, in the end, eaten a dinner of toast and cereal and a glass of warm milk? Let alone the nod, how about a simple turn of her head to show him that she could feel him looking at her? Look at her, without even panties left on, bending over the tub, the seam of her ass curving down on where her legs opened. He had eyes. He could see everything right down to the pucker of skin that hung unevenly. Without so much as a nod or a glance to say that any of it was for him, the way she bent down lower to finger the water and the pucker broke just a nibble open.

Come on! The house, the boy, the split of her legs, wasn't any of it actually his?

Imagine it, her bending over herself with a blade of some kind, getting at all of it, cutting it down to what she had cut it down to. And where would the boy have been? Was that really even a question? No doubt right there, right beside her, where the boy always was, watching her shave or cut or whatever at it.

Or, imagine this—the boy down in the tub looking up at her cutting it. The boy was probably right there, down in the tub looking right up at it, her one leg lifted up on the tub lip so that she could get at it all with the blade. Just imagine the boy watching the hairs dropping and sticking on the sides of the tub.

What was she thinking? He would like to know. She was not thinking about him, he could bet on that. She had not so much as asked him if he would like it—her all shaved down to look like some kind of girl again. Who was she trying to fool?

She might be able to fool some fool of a kid, but, please, that was about it.

Those old wrinkled lips.

Please! He had seen it all stretched out.

There was no forgetting that.

He would tell the boy.

He would just walk right up behind her and get what was properly his.

It was his.

He would take it properly, all right.

Isn't this what she was asking for?

For him to do his job. Tell the boy what and how it was. Then have her the old way.

Yes, sir, he was back.

AHOY

This is the story of the year my wife became the sea captain's wife and carried his child, a child that is by all rights mine.

My wife is wildly, crazily, ridiculously, fucked-uppedly beautiful.

It's insane but she's almost more beautiful in the bonnet and linen-spun gown she walks through town wearing on her way to and from the Captain's house.

I can't imagine how this must sound.

If you're married, I'm counting on you having at least come to the minor revelation of how little we know inside another marriage. And maybe, wherever you are in your own marriage—crossing a rainy parking lot on your way to the office or coming at night to your front door—with a sharp, embarrassed flash or a longing you can't quite name, you've wondered what you really know about the house you're about to enter, about your own marriage?

"Olivia," I said this morning. She stood at the gate leading up to the Captain's house. She straightened the apron that covered her gown. Her once-slender waist is gone. She ties the apron strings high, just under her very full breasts. Even under the thickness of the layered skirt, I could make out the tight roundness of her belly. The pregnancy looked like part of the period costume. She stared up the street with a hopeful look. I said her name again and it was clear that she was not trying to avoid me. I simply didn't exist.

In some weird way, I know it wasn't personal. Most of what is called daily life, or modern life, seems to have disappeared for Olivia. I can't even say I'm a ghost to her—since how could I be a twenty-first-century ghost when she's in the nineteenth century?

Let me say, plain and as sober as I can manage, the fact that we even came to the island is my fault. Corny, sure. Okay, damn ironic, given how things went. I've always harbored romantic notions of a life by the sea. Guess my major in college. I was the guy at the dinner party belting out Wordsworth's warning, *Getting and spending, we lay waste our powers.* Despite growling a couple lofty sonnets, I hadn't gone on for the PhD, instead availing myself of the Internet boon, hooking up with my definitely smarter, more practical friends, creating the proverbial start-up—and then, with some skill and luck, riding the wave and selling off to a bigger, badder corporation. Whatever other apologies I give down the line, the ride was a blast. Quite a hot-shit ride. I don't think I need to talk figures. It left us flush.

Olivia and I had been out to dinner when I brought up the island. The restaurant was new, its look new—kind of high-industrial-meets-French-château, heavy on design. Lots of serious steel-beam work. Big, dangle-burdened chandeliers. The damn food came out on steel plates, like something you'd display on a mantelpiece.

"Come on, it'll be an adventure," I begged. "Baby, enough of all this shit, aren't we a little sick of it?" I said, looking around the room, putting my hand up to say no to the gaggle of waiters who hovered, ready to respond to our every breath. "Let's just go." I railed about how we'd become people who spent Saturday nights in loser pretentious restaurants, so deep in my riff that I tossed my napkin down on the table as if I were ready to take off right then.

"I want my entrée," my wife said, rolling the *r* with exaggerated Frenchliness just to let me know she thought I'd gone overboard. I tried a softer tactic. Sorry, I really was sorry for everything I'd dragged her though these last years. We'd both known what was involved. Name me a start-up that doesn't have the ground-level team pretty much camping out 24-7 in the office. High risk, big yield. Net result for us—good money, real safety—but I told Olivia that I knew how far away it had taken us from each other. I was ready to make it worth her patience by stepping away, going to live in our summer place off-season and plan together for a great what-next.

"Come with me, Olivia," I said, like I was back down on my knees asking her to be my wife. "Come away with me," I said with biblical flourish.

She lifted her wine glass to put something between us. It was clear she felt that I was cheap, using the abrasion of our marriage during the work frenzy as a negotiating point. She took a sip and gave the slightest shake of her head.

"We're really okay," she said.

"Come on," I said, "tell me what could be so terribly wrong with a year where I cook for you, we take long walks, maybe we both learn to watercolor? Maybe we'll come away wanting a whole different kind of life."

My wife leaned across the metal table, touching my face with her hand. This is a particular gesture she makes, this light touch of her fingers—tender and serious at once—a gesture that says her attention is entirely focused and that whatever she will say next is something she wants me to attend to seriously.

"I like our life," she said, her hand stilled against my face like punctuation. "You want watercolor, Brian, take watercolor at Mass Art."

She looked at me, and, though she'd pretty much flat out rejected my idea, I felt a wave of extraordinary luckiness. Or maybe it was just the charge from knowing I was going to have to muscle up for the win. My wife's not easily convinced. I like that about her. She comes at new ideas skeptically, all of her intent on finding the chip, the flaw, any hidden error, before she signs on with her enthusiasm, which is always worth the skepticism.

"We could work on the baby." I pressed my hand over her hand and held her steady gaze.

She pulled her hand from my face, sat way back in the silk-upholstered steel chair. "Fine. Here I am," she said and looked at me like a dark dare.

"I mean out there, out at the beach."

"Boston's a fine place to work on having a baby. Many people work on babies in the city." She put the emphasis on *work*.

Maybe it was as simple as having offended her by calling it work. Maybe I'd played a big card too fast, or maybe right up front I'd played *the* big card. We weren't the last of our friends to do the baby thing, but we were definitely on the back side of the whole family extravaganza. Some were doing their second. I'd been the reluctant one. The one saying, Hey, let's wait a little more. It's not that I didn't want a baby. I did, kind of. I just didn't really want what I saw as life with a baby. And not just the whole slew of bouncing, rocking, whistling junk my friends carted around every time they deigned to wreak havoc on the sacred nap schedule and meet up for brunch. It was supposedly a real benefit for a couple, the whole life's-richer-with-kids project, but the way it looked in my friends' marriages, I couldn't figure out who benefited, and if we couldn't get a bigger return investing in something else.

I realize that talking about other couples—their romantic and domestic mess-ups, their drooling babies—makes it look like I'm avoiding the big elephant I rode right into this New England front parlor at the start. Can you blame me? It has been months now that, passing my wife, I say her name, Olivia, and she doesn't turn or show the slightest recognition. Not even annoyance.

I am instead wholly unimagined.

End of July, we came out to the island. We brought books, art supplies, enough imported first-press olive oil to get us through the year. We left all birth control back in the bathroom cupboard. Obviously, I'd won. The details of those negotiations seem irrelevant now, though I've obviously proven I'm not the best judge of what's relevant. Plan was, we'd come for summer season and then check in. She'd reserved the right to say no. I wouldn't be permitted to launch a new campaign.

August was a blast. Like a college summer, but without a flimsy summer job. No deals to close. No late hours. Nothing. And way better than a college summer, because now we had the dough to really party. And that's pretty much what we did. Before heading into my back-to-the-basics of reading poetry and watercoloring, I had partying to get in and money to burn. I want to emphasize this: we both did the burning. Olivia was into it, my beautiful, beautiful party girl, wearing gauzy dresses to clambakes, and because it was high summer or we'd just come straight from swimming, a lot of time she wore these practically sheer cotton sheaths with nothing underneath.

"You're going like that?" I'd ask, but Olivia could see I hardly cared, or, better, I liked the daring that had come over her since we'd come to the island. Not that anyone could call Olivia prim or prudish, just that there was a kind of greater freedom in her, a naturalness that was breathtaking. I might see her perched on the flat armrest of an Adirondack chair, leaning into one of the other men in a way that was sexy—not like she was inviting trouble or wanting any escalation; her body just seemed true. I didn't feel jealous. I never thought she was trying to make me feel jealous. If I thought of anything much—and with the drinking and some of the drugs I'd dipped into, okay, my thinking was already questionable—I thought she was gaining a kind of purity, a lightness, a sort of back-to-nature thing that worked for me—and for my hope that she'd let August turn into the winter adventure I wanted.

At night, or dawn, back in our house, I'd lift her dress off in a fast sweep. "That's my girl," I'd say, and she'd growl something back at me. Other nights, we crashed in our clothes, and during the early hours when I'd wake, ridiculously thirsty and full of silent repentant promises, I'd untangle her dress and slip it off her damp body. "Thanks," she'd whisper, and I'd say, "Drink up," giving Olivia a glass of water. "I need this," she'd say, and I'd say, "Yes, I know," and then curl behind my wife, glad to have given her this simple thing she needed.

∽

"You're the best summer fling I ever had," I told Olivia. It was afternoon, classic late-August light, languorous, stolen time, the best hours, we'd agreed, for lovemaking, and we'd been making love on and off for the whole afternoon. The drapes slapped quietly with the wind.

"What happens when summer's over?" she asked, rolling onto her stomach, pretending a bit of hurt, but I knew she was just trying to provoke me with the dip of her back and curve of her ass.

"Oh, then I must go back to my wife," I said.

"Your wife?" she sat up with a start, gathering the sheet as if suddenly stunned into modesty. It had been a game up till then. But when I slowly unwrapped her from the sheet and pulled her on top of me, something had changed and I wanted her to know. "Yes," I whispered, "I love my wife. I love my wife more than I will ever begin to be able to tell her."

"I have a husband, too, you know," she said. It sounded like a painful confession.

"Do you love him?" I asked. I can't say exactly why, but I felt nervous about how she'd answer. I couldn't tell if she knew that I'd shifted, that I was way out of the make-believe. She was slow to answer. She found sand still stuck on my shoulder and brushed it off. Then she propped herself up, sphinx-like above me, and kept looking at me.

"Do you love him?" It came out in barely a whisper.

"I do, very much. Sometimes I think I've needed this fling with you to remind me just how much I love him."

I kissed her and she kissed me back deeply, and I thought that we had said something essential to one another, something that was a pledge, almost a renewal of vows.

Most days now, I follow Olivia along the shore road. Yesterday was bitter cold. I layered in thermal-this and thermal-that, packing extra warmth with my flask, while Olivia was barely wrapped in a knitted shawl. I worry about her and the baby. She kept to the shoulder of the road. Most of the houses along the shore are boarded for winter; it isn't unusual to go the whole two miles without a car passing. If she caught sight of me, hopping between the rocks and the shore trees, swigging from the flask, hiding behind a pine when she stopped and stood star-ing, she never let on.

Yesterday it occurred to me that my wife is like the beautiful woman in the John Fowles novel, *The French Lieutenant's Woman*. I tried to remember what I could about that book. For example, whether it comes to a good end. But all I recalled was the woman in a cape in some godforsaken rocky coastal village, and that, like Olivia, she comes to a promontory and stares out to sea. There's a man, maybe a couple men. She stands and stares and pines for the French Lieutenant as Olivia does for the Captain. Along the way, there's obsession, maybe more than one person's obsession. I determined the novel might be useful and that I should go back and have a reread.

For all my wanting to live the calm island life, I had a hard time slowing down, even after the summer mayhem quieted into September and September was, I learned, the great secret summer month, clear perfect walking days, or days to set up and paint outdoors. But the watercolor thing wasn't happening. I was barely reading, barely getting myself out to walk in the low dunes. Some nights I cooked us a good meal, but by the time dinner was ready, I'd gone through a bottle of wine and had no stomach for food. I was drinking like I was still at a big outdoor summer party and—fuck, what's to lose, I'll just say it—I was keeping up with the blow. Not every day, but still, most days I was doing lines, something I hadn't indulged in back in college or even with my partners, who, more times than not, did a bump before important meetings.

Olivia stopped pretty quickly with our little drug foray. She'd started taking yoga in the church basement and she said she didn't have to be the Dalai Lama to figure out that doing sun salutations the morning after you've practically snorted your way to a heart attack didn't make a whole lot of sense. I told her I'd stopped too. All the more for me, is what I thought, and I carried on. "Here's to the journey," I'd whisper, bending over a fat line, like I was a Carlos Castaneda disciple, half believing it really was some kind of toxic soul cleanse, better than Olivia's pretentious yoga practice. Look, I told Olivia whatever shit I told her and I told myself whatever shit I told myself and then I'd hoover a fatty, swiping my finger along the table to smear the residue on my gums.

It was late in August that Olivia first started at Hardwick House. First she filled in for a woman from the yoga class who worked as a tour guide, and when the woman didn't come back after a week, Olivia stayed on. She'd made a commitment to the Captain's House through the New Year, when tours terminated for the season.

"It's pretty interesting," she said. "Come on, I've got to do something more than yoga and lobster if you want me to stay on here all winter." She was pinning up her hair to fit under the bonnet.

"Sick of lobster already?" I said, pressing myself against the back of her long dress. I was glad she was planning into the winter. I slipped my hands tightly around her waist.

"Like a sailor who's been at sea for a year," she said, pressing back.

"Your husband had been planning a lobster-sherry bisque for dinner. Perhaps he'll skip lobster and yield to sherry."

"What a major surprise, this husband." She gathered her skirts and rushed off for the midday tour. Fuck her and her fucking annoyance, I thought, her patronizing holier-than-thou, sudden teetotaler attitude. If I couldn't have my summer Olivia back, then I wasn't unhappy to have her out of the house for the day and not throwing me any of these funky concerned looks when I refilled a tumbler or disappeared into the bathroom to do a bump.

Now I wonder whom Olivia even meant when she spoke of her husband. How invisible was I already to my wife?

I've asked what we know about the marriages of even our closest friends. My wife would say, if she were still at all inclined to speak of such things, that she knew a whole lot about our friends' marriages.

"Women talk," she used to say to me.

"About what?" I'd ask, ready for her to make me horny.

"You're ridiculously transparent." She'd pretend to be offended.

"Then peek in the window," I'd say, already hard.

Sometimes it might go that way. She wasn't above describing the way one friend liked her thick nipples squeezed as she jazzed up to her climax, or some technique a friend had tried out that Olivia was ready to try out on me. I knew whose wife had gone full Brazilian as a Valentine's gift. Pretty quickly, the stories went the stupid way she knew I wanted them to go. With me as the best lover, hot husband, one with the biggest dick—straight-out stupid guy shit. But who's not aching for just that? Anyway, it was a kind of game we played, not that we really needed our friends' lives to get us going. Just hearing her talk dirty, saying *nipple* or *juicy*—or maybe it was the idea that women do that: trade techniques, tell one another about their guys' moves—that was exciting.

Sometimes it backfired and she'd get all serious, even a little angry, and then, even though it wasn't our marriage under scrutiny, it was as if I'd done something wrong.

"Can you believe it?" she said, describing Patricia's hurt over the way Theo had never once in all the years kissed Patricia when he walked through the front door.

"Maybe he didn't want to be obvious," I said, feeling off the hook, since I loved kissing Olivia everywhere—doorways, pet stores, at traffic lights.

"We're not talking flowers," she said, looking contemptuous. "Or lovemaking at the threshold. We're talking the basic hey-babe peck before changing into sweatpants. It's Marriage 101."

"You did good getting me." I knew I'd made a mistake even before she gave me that look—the one that says, how pathetic, how unkind and selfish and, well, *how male.*

"And when did this become about you?"

I knew better than to try to take it back or say something about how I'd always believed Theo wasn't good enough for Patricia, since anything I'd say was bound to be wrong, further proof that even though I kissed my wife everyday, I was really just like Theo, a Theo-in-disguise, and that my kisses were as wrong-minded as his absent kisses. Suddenly our whole dinner conversation became a deep crevasse, and I'd have to read the topographic map of her emotions, trying to figure out which way to take it: sometimes she wanted to be called on her shit, wanted me to kind of plow her down, even literally; sometimes, it was best to tackle her, wrestle like squabbling playground mates; and sometimes it was better to let her rage around until she could make her way back to me.

❧

That look I saw on Olivia—her eyes cast down the street in what, as a nod to the 1800s, I'm calling her countenance, that smooth, anticipatory glance—has come to be Olivia's look, as if she's keeping keen to the possibility that the Captain's ship might return this very day to the port. According to her—to the journal book left on the writing table in the Captain's House—he's been away for seven months. The dates of his leaving pretty much coincide with Olivia's taking up the guide position at the house and also, calculating backward, to her pregnancy.

The Captain's House is a restored colonial, once home to Captain Hardwick. The Island Historical Society purchased the home after it fell into disrepair, restoring it closely to its original state. Now for three-quarters of the year it's open; tours run three times a day, detailing nineteenth-century life through the lens of a sea captain and the town where he resided. The tour is done living-history-style like Plimoth Plantation and Mystic Seaport, the tour guide assuming a name and a historical identity. Apparently, for a while the house was staffed by a man who alternated identities between the town miller and Captain Hardwick himself, as though recently returned from a trip to the East Indies. And so it was that Olivia, when she took over for her yoga friend, became the Captain's wife. The odd, uncanny thing was that though the Captain's wife was actually Hannah Hardwick, in all their marital correspondence she's referred to exclusively by her middle name, Olivia.

"I am Olivia Hardwick, welcome. Unfortunately, the Captain is at sea, so he will not be able to personally greet you—though he trusts that I will well see after your concerns and inquiries," she'd say to a group crowded in the parlor of the house.

The tour groups were predictable. On rainy days, they'd stand in sorry, dripping ponchos, sullen teenagers plugged into their machines, some kid already whining, "I'm hungry," before Olivia had even finished her first phrase.

"How do you do it?" I challenged after the first time I went on the tour. "Don't you want to kill them?"

"I don't mind," she said. "It is fine to have company whilst the Captain is away."

"Oh, the good Captain doesn't mind our visits?" I teased. "Let's go back up to the bedchamber; there is something to which we might give closer attentions."

Olivia flashed her don't-be-such-an-idiot look. She opened the hutch, busying herself dusting shelves of pottery. When she turned, she seemed genuinely surprised that I was still there. "Go, Brian, get out please. I've got to plan for the afternoon; there's a special private tour of the Hardwick scrimshaw collection."

I didn't get out. I hung around while she got ready for the private tour. I made easy fun of stupid tourists and smart-assed that I had a big sperm-whale tooth for her to scrimshaw. I told her how impressive it was, all she'd learned about the whaling period, but if I sounded patronizing, I figured I'd earned it, since I not only knew my whaling history, but had actually introduced Olivia to that part of American history.

It wasn't only English Romanticism that had occupied me in college; I'd been taken by the Americans: Thoreau, Melville, Whitman, and Emerson. But the romance of the American worker—sailors, builders, miners, glassblowers—was something that more than once I had carried on about in serious blowhard fashion. I thought my ideas were hugely original. My senior thesis had been a literary analysis of American work music. Shanties, ballads, their links to the Child Ballads. During our courtship, I'd dragged poor Olivia on a tour of New England historical homes, driving from Maine to Connecticut, sometimes visiting two, even three sites a day. If she suffered that time, she did so with such grace that I can't even conjure an annoyed glance or a time she came up with an excuse and waited for me back in the bed-and-breakfast.

When I proposed to her, I did so in the Concord graveyard. I couldn't imagine anything more perfect than to ask Olivia to make our lives together surrounded by the spirits and gravestones of my intellectual mentors buried on the rise of the graveyard. She walked away from me. I took it as an indication of her being overwhelmed by feeling. I was too. The afternoon light slanted down through the blue pines. It was reverent light. I could see she was crying. I pulled myself up from my kneeling position and went over to her. I saw us as being in some beautiful dance right then, the sunlight breaking against a tree. I paced myself, ready to come up behind her and repeat everything I'd said with her folded in my arms. But as I approached, she turned away.

"You're an asshole. And yes, I'll marry you," she said and kept walking, not stopping till she got back to where we'd parked the car. She didn't speak until we were back in our first, small apartment in Boston.

"Say it now." She stood in the middle of our living room. "Can you say it here? Just here in this regular apartment with our brand-new toaster and television and the rest of our stupid life accumulating around us."

I had no clue what she was in a tizzy about. I couldn't imagine anything better than what I'd done. If we could have married right there, in that graveyard among the graves of the Transcendentalists, I would have considered it our greatest marital blessing.

I've been sketching out the roughs for my new venture, a program that at first I called WouldaCouldaShoulda. Screw a rough sketch. The idea alone should generate quick seed-funding. Like any perfect risk, any genuine innovation, it's simple—so, likewise, I've simplified the name and now I'm calling it Hindsight. Not only does it allow a person to project ahead—incorporating how particular personalities invariably react to actions and words, setting out subsequent long-term consequences—but more importantly, with a simple click, the technology provides suitable alternatives. Forget about the obvious financial or political possibilities of such an application. Hindsight is a boon to our personal lives.

No more wishing you'd done it differently. No more fucking up. All personal data, downloaded; the data of all friends, colleagues, family relations, downloaded. Then, just type in an action, press the return button, and see the aftermath of a decision. Or the application actually listens in on a conversation, let's say between husband and wife, and it does the work you refuse to do—it actually listens, for the flat-out lie, for the barb, the subtle jab, for what she is actually saying—and then it clearly outlines possible alternative actions and the consequences of not shifting the conversation's direction or simply stopping and acknowledging, "I'm sorry. Let me take that back. It was an idiotic thing to say. I'd like to understand what you're saying."

One afternoon in early September, Olivia burst onto the sunporch, yanking the paper from my hand. I blinked open, fumbled for the paper, hoping she hadn't exactly caught me nodding off, and pretended she'd interrupted my reading.

Olivia bent over me, hand on my cheek in the way I've already described, looking at me with such open, clean happiness. "I'm pregnant."

"Well, what a tart and a wench you turned out to be." I goosed her through her layered linen skirts. She was still in the Hardwick House tour costume. "How'd you get with child? Sailor or captain?" I was an idiot, and worse, even half tanked, I knew it right off. Even an idiot's smart enough not to joke when he learns his wife is pregnant. But I was too fucked up to care; I was two bloody marys into the *Sunday Week in Review*, and though I was in running clothes, I hadn't gone running. I was drunk, dozed off, and it was Wednesday. At least, I thought it was probably Wednesday. The burst of her onto the sunporch, the blast of her suddenly there, joyous, flushed with a future, our future, came like a punch.

I needed to block and strike.

I kept at her. "You're speechless, lass? Or don't you know if that would be Captain or Cook that put you with child?"

"That would be my husband," she said, already out the door, calling back, "You needn't worry, Brian, you were just a charming summer fuck."

I should have run after her but I stayed on the porch, slowly finishing my drink, slowly finishing the *Week in Review*. I took my ridiculous, foolish, pathetic, asshole time before I went inside and found Olivia curled on our bed. She looked up at me. "I don't even know you anymore."

Did I say I'm sorry? Did I lie next to her on the bed and tell her how happy the news of our child made me? Did I do anything other than say, "Have fun with your captain. He'll offer a great life," and walk out of the bedroom?

Of course I didn't. Hey, hey, I'm the CEO and poster boy for Hindsight.

Olivia took to the nineteenth century. Natural soap, local produce—it initially looked less like historical reenactment than like respect for the environment, a questioning of materialism that echoed the back to the Wordsworthian ideology I'd been running on at the mouth about. I thought she was trying to show just what a good camper she was, show me that I'd been right. Her way of saying, I'm here, just where you wanted me, now come join me. She cleaned the house of processed foods. She wouldn't wear anything synthetic. Then I figured it was an accommodation for the pregnancy, since even when you're not asking, there's practically a national broadcast a day about chemicals and shit we use daily having lasting effects on the fetus.

It made me hungry for Doritos and Cheez Wiz.

It made me want to sneak to the bathroom and cut a double ski trail, with a vodka chaser.

It made me think my fucking pregnant wife was trying to make me feel guilty for having a little fun after years of working 24-7-and-a-half to make us financially safe.

But there was also a weird shift in her language. It's not that Olivia had ever had my level of trash mouth, but it wasn't shocking to hear her say *what the fuck* or *fuck you*. Between us, when things got going, she could be good and explicit. But that afternoon on the porch was the last time I've heard her curse. Even a simple *damn it, Brian* never punctuated her mistakes as she knitted—and, hello!—there was knitting, something she'd taken up as she began learning her way into whaling history and the life in Hardwick House. It wasn't just knitting; she took to making tallow candles and using oil lamps when the dusk came on. I didn't reform; I didn't give up white flour. I didn't pull out the watercolors or the Wordsworth. I said I was celebrating, which meant brooding, useless and drunk before lunch.

I've never understood it when a guy says, "We're pregnant." What the fuck is that about? Some guilty asshole looking for sensitivity brownie points? And I've never understood why any woman would stand sharing the credit for the crazy, serious work of growing a baby inside her body. Olivia was with me on that. In fact, it seemed from the first that it was important I acknowledge that she was the one puking and repulsed at the smell of coffee, just for starters.

The only thing I managed to do to acknowledge her pregnancy was to read the two books Olivia ordered, *What to Expect When You're Expecting* and another book that gave day-by-day descriptions of the fetus's development, a book of such terrifying explicitness I could hardly stand to look at Olivia, knowing what could be going wrong inside her body. It spooked me so much just to conjure the growing baby's spine and heart that I could only read the book in daylight and then only secretly, while Olivia was out taking her daily walk to get fresh milk from a local farm, or when she went off to the Hardwick House.

There are obvious questions. What the fuck happened that a perfectly sane, bright woman believes herself to be living in the mid-1800s? Or that I spend my days drunk and hiding behind trees while Olivia wears a bonnet and stares out to sea?

At first, it was obvious that the problem was mine. Right after I learned Olivia was pregnant, we started in on some nasty fighting. We'd never been fighters and now we fought a lot. It didn't help that I was usually so wasted on a lazy Susan of drinks and blow and then a fist of pills and more drinks to ease me down from the blow that I was a ragged fuse.

I don't remember hitting Olivia, but apparently I hit her good and hard. This was early and there was a visit to the island clinic to check if she and the baby were all in one piece. There was a lame story about the tub and the doctor saying that apart from nasty bruising everyone was fine but did she want to tell him anything else and her looking hard at me and saying no, nothing else for now. And while now I see—another pretty obvious wouldacouldashoulda—that it would have been best for Olivia to have called the cops, made me deal with my shit then and there, instead she just took off and spent the next few nights in the Captain's House. I won't go through the whole thing about those couple of days right now—what I promised, the shame I felt. Suffice it to say she came back. She was wary and distant, but she'd been that way since the day on the porch.

I took it as a new challenge. If I knew anything, it was how to aggressively work in the face of a slumping market. Never look like you're yielding. Always come at it game-on. So I eased off the drinking, pulled out the watercolors, and it looked, at least for a few weeks, like things could be okay. I started running, convincing myself the cold air felt good as it tore through my throat. I asked Olivia questions about the pregnancy and cooked her nutrient-rich meals with local kale and beets. I made a big show of having a single cocktail at night.

I asked Olivia if she'd let me paint her.

"That's lovely," she said. "With a book, or this?" She pointed to the shawl she was then knitting. The one she now wraps herself in for her daily walks.

I suggested a pose where her still mostly flat belly would be just a little visible, perhaps poked up through the tub water, revealing the promise and hint of a swell as she lay naked in the tub, reading.

"Without clothes?" she said, as if I'd said something so prepos-
terous as to actually be funny.

I swaggered toward her, attempting my best painter-in-the-stu-
dio-with-lovely-model affect, and stood leeringly close to Olivia, making breathy French exclamations.

"Ooh là là." I pawed at her sweater, crimping it down to expose
a shoulder and her much delightfully fuller breast. "This fecund beauty
must be immortalized by me." I hoped we could slip into one of the
little pretend games we enjoyed. It would be good for both of us. We
were so far from the easy play of our summer pleasures. I'd read in
her books that some women become quite frightened of sexual contact
during pregnancy, while others are eager, highly aroused right up until
labor. Really, I was nervous too. Everything about my wife seemed a
little foreign—the dark line that I'd read might suddenly appear like a
painted stroke down her stomach, the browning and widening of her
nipples. At some point, a book said, I might touch her nipples and a
thin, premilk fluid would bead up. Already, Olivia seemed less exotic
than inhabited, occupied. Pregnancy seemed like an infection, an aggressive symptom.

"Please stop," she shouted, no coy hint of playful in her voice.

"But your beauty, ma chére," I leered and squeezed her heavy breast. "Such lush fruit."

She swatted me away, grabbing up her sweater. Olivia glared, her head shaking. She recoiled as if she'd actually been skunked.

"What's your fucking problem?" I said.

She picked up her knitting needles and began working with furious, jabbing motions. I stood waiting for her to say anything, for her to blast off one of her snarky rebuttals. Even to shoot me her bullet stink-eye, a leave-me-alone-Brian-or-I'll-bite-your-dick-off glance that meant that I was looking at an emotional topo map I knew how to manage. Instead, Olivia looked scared.

"What's your fucking problem?" I said and threw my brush down so it splattered across the thick, pebbly paper.

The journal I've mentioned is kept open on the small desk in the Hardwick parlor. But now that the Hardwick has closed for the season, Olivia keeps it on a small desk she has set for herself in our spare bedroom. The entries are mostly domestic—a close record of household expenses, her encounters with people she calls shopkeepers or merchants. In addition to the daily purchases and costs, she often notes an observation, as in, *The Miller Goodwin is a most courteous man, always wishing me health and noting my high color.* The entries are never entirely without some basis in reality; the man who runs the island's year-round health-food store where we buy flour in bulk is, indeed, Tim Goodwin.

There is mention of a drunk, a noisome poor soul who lurches pitifully through town: *I should not say beyond saving, my Captain, but if you were to see his disrepair I fear even you might agree.*

A tribute, no doubt. An invitation to pour myself a shot.

The journal also serves as a record of the pregnancy, though less a record of her body's changes than a delighted recounting of the antics of Annabelle or Josiah. She calls the child inside Annabelle or Josiah, referring to the baby almost as if it has already been born. She writes, *Captain, how proud you would be today! Our Annabelle kicked and bullied me as I went about chores. She is a fierce girl, if perhaps a bit stubborn already. I sang so that she would not feel lonely as I moved about. And though I know it isn't possible, I am certain that her kicking began to find tempo with my singing. She'll be a great delight to the Captain. His bonnie Annabelle. Oh how it must grieve him to be so far from his baby. I must be ever more attentive so that I might recount these months as vividly as if he were right beside his little girl.*

The next day it might be about his stalwart Josiah: *Captain, your boy is a rascally boy already quite ready for the sea. He dances a jig against my ribs. He juts always leeward, threatening to capsize his poor mother.*

And then there are the passages of longing for the Captain, exquisite, private moments where she speaks to him directly. She worries about weather, and the great distance, and the many dangers he faces at sea, and then chastises herself for any bad thoughts, encouraging lightness and joy, and then, always, the closing lines, *I hold you, my Captain, close to my heart, Your ever always devoted, Olivia.*

Was it by early January that the Captain began to send word?

By what means did the letters arrive, a new one stacked weekly on top of a slender bundle she tied with yarn and kept beside her journal? It did not seem that Olivia ever questioned how they arrived. *I shall try to keep you close by endeavoring at every opportunity to sketch what I encounter in port or on the high sea,* Captain Hardwick penned in tidy script. Of a squall, he described how *the light squall rose rapidly windward of the ship.* He gave orders: *The men were quick as they had only minutes to draw the light sails before the blast was down upon us. Such a fury of the elements we must contend with.*

His letters were so tender—*All my life I have loved the sea, yet now the vast sea cannot compare with the affection that stirs within for you, Olivia—devoted—Even the unaccountably numerous stars, the abundant, beautifully hued fish, the various birds could not tempt a captain to linger along these temperate islands a moment longer than is absolutely mandatory, when what awaits his return home is my darling Olivia—concerned—How do you manage these cold months? I fear I have not left ample supply of wood or oil for lamps. I wish each day only that I could know you are healthy and strong.* Sometimes, despite his resolve, he became melancholic—*I fear, my good wife, that I might never see you again, though I refuse to harbor such thoughts for long and instead endeavor to turn my attentions to the fate of my crew and the success of my journey.*

I read and reread the letters perhaps as many times as Olivia. As she went out for her chores, I'd sit in the hard-back desk chair and pull the yarn string, watching the bow unfurl. I smelled the paper, the rich walnut ink. I'd toast the Captain with a tumbler of dark rum. I held each letter, not with the private shame of a cuckolded husband so much as with a kind of voyeurism, as if I actually felt in my hands the anticipation my wife felt opening a newly arrived missive, lingering over a phrase, letting herself relish the emotion behind the Captain's words.

My Olivia, it occurs to me today that I have provoked undue

hardship upon you, offering only the harsh existence of a captain's wife.
Would you have consented, knowing the lonely months that awaited
you? Perhaps I would have been slight company for one as cultivated.
And though others might long to linger in these temperate waters or fill
their coffers with bounty from these rich and exotic shores, I push my
men, perhaps too rigorously, in every effort to fill our barrels with oil and
return expeditiously. You are the star, my guiding star, always. You are
the shore, the beacon I hasten toward. No doubt I will return to you a
man weakened and scudded by the angry seas. Forgive me, Olivia—

I was moved to tears. Big tears smudged the ink; the finely
scripted letters ran. I licked the ink. "Oh Captain," I sobbed, salt, ink
and rum thick on my tongue.

Olivia takes her shore-road walk and comes, finally, to where the road
dead ends. She makes her way out onto the rocky peninsula. She's grown
large, and though I should rush to help since the rocks are sharp and
slick with kelp, I creep close and stay hidden behind a boulder.

She stares out at the Atlantic. I drink from my flask and stare
at her. The wind is strong and noisy, and from my crouched distance, I
can't make out what she says. I watch her lips move while she reads the
new letter from Captain Hardwick. I imagine she already recites this

new letter by heart. *I'd like to bring home an emerald parrot to brighten our New England parlor.* Inside her, the baby at seven months listens, I think, to mother's voice. *Would that pretty talking bird bring happiness, my dearest, when I am away these long months?* Then she pulls her shawl tight and stares back toward the horizon, where I believe she conjures gaily dressed native men and women buying pineapples and guavas in tropical island markets. Does the baby who by now has all five senses, who the books say feels the mother's moods, does the baby share Olivia's longing?

"Let him die at sea," I shout from behind my boulder.

Just as I can't hear her, the shore winds and waves slapping against the promontory make it impossible for Olivia to hear my rants.

I tip the flask and cry out, "Let the ocean waves roll and break piece by wooden piece his damn schooner! Let him die of scurvy and die again of equatorial tsetse fly flu. Let him die a long exacting syphilitic death after rum-soaked nights in the company of mermaids and cabin boys."

I rant and cry and belch.

She stands and stares. Her graceful fingers stroke the thin letter paper. Oh, I've gotten myself in a high lather, stringing a drunken sailor's worth of curses at the Captain. My heart is mutinous.

❧

Fuck it all, I have so little left to lose—or is it that only by losing every-thing I might actually begin—so let this whole story unfurl.

This is from all the way back in the fall, in October, I can't track so well anymore, but maybe around when Olivia went silent.

Anyway, there was Susan, a wretched and newly divorced prin-cess I'd taken to meeting in the afternoons. Predictable and pitiful, I knew that, which served only to make me say stupid, pitiful insipidities to her, like "I want this happiness to last."

Or I'd say, "This isn't going to end well, princess," as if mention-ing the inevitable made me prescient.

"It isn't going well already," Susan laughed, leaning over her granite kitchen island. She was sleeveless and recklessly tan, ramping up for her postdivorce madness.

Mostly I was afraid she'd scatter the blow by laughing. I wanted her to hurry the fuck up so I could get to my line.

"Who would have guessed?" she'd say, as if acting like a mid-dle-aged idiot was original. But Susan knew she was a little pitiful too, which made her feel dear and akin to me, thus poetic and worthwhile.

She was living her first winter on the island in the house she'd won in her settlement. There was a sort-of-actual boyfriend, a white kid with dreadlocks and bongos, who took the weekend ferry out and left Mondays with cash for a new supply of Bolivian. Mostly it was an opportunity for me to lean over Susan's granite counter.

Other things happened. Predictable, frantic, not very success-ful coked-up couplings. Big surprise. I didn't need some desperate next-day epiphany or the dreaded walk home to Olivia at an hour later than a husband should be coming home to a pregnant wife with a bullshit story of where I'd been for me to feel shitty, though I managed to twist it so I felt mostly shitty for myself. I'd like to say I got it at least together enough to end the consorting.

But sometime before Halloween, the weekend boyfriend, like a stoned jack-o'-lantern, stayed on, and after another week, Susan and Bongo Dreadlock started talking about Jamaica for the winter. By the next week they'd gone vegan, sober, cleansing juices up the wazoo, Bongo Dreadlock spewing manifestos on coke as the devil incarnate and weed as the fucking savior of western civilization. Susan mussed his hair, kissed him, any shred of irony gone from her conversation. She hung on his every word like he was Bob fucking Marley. Without blow or Susan's gay divorcée attitude of if-it's-wrong-let-me-do-it, it was all pretty much over. By then, anyway, I was mostly ready to buckle down for a long winter and drink in my own home, thank you very much.

So there, fine, fuck it, that's everything. You could say we're even, Olivia and I, when it comes to straying from our marriage.

I was not made to feel welcome this afternoon at the library. More than once, the sorry bitch of a librarian cut close to the children's table, where I'd parked myself. This is not the first she's seen of me. I come to read and check out books. She might not approve of me, but the library is public. It is my right. She lingered, peering over my shoulder, certain that I, this season's notable drunk, was up to no malingering good. I have been accused of being up to behaviors not fit for a public library. Sleeping in the stacks, cursing at gossiping fools—I'm a public nuisance. Accused of attempting to make off with books not properly checked out, I shouted, "False, false!" The stupid bitch librarian knows anyone might make such a simple error.

I felt her behind me, shivering with anticipation, awaiting any slight misdeed. I showed her. I did not so much as take a nip from my fortifications and kept them properly out of her snooping sight. I had a tidy pile of books. A book on scrimshaw treasures, another on scrimshaw techniques, *The French Lieutenant's Woman*, and an absolute treasure of a book I found some months ago called *Incidents of a Whaling Voyage* by Frances Allyn Olmsted, a book, incidentally, predating Melville's monster by ten years.

Why the children's table? *The child is the father of Man*, declares my Wordsworth. I am ready. Each day more ready. I want a child's wonder. Let Olivia know I am ready for this child to be my guide, my full sail.

Today I did a quick skim of the Fowles novel. Actually, I'd found the CliffsNotes in the library. Isn't right, is it? What kind of library has CliffsNotes shelved next to the actual book? In any case, given what the CliffsNotes calls Fowles's "subject of the novel," the artist's relationship with his creation, and his "technique" of playing with novel conventions, I think Mr. Fowles would find it amusing to see his big old novel open and me at the children's table, hiding CliffsNotes inside. Fouling with Fowles. Very twentieth century. Meta, very meta.

Then, behold behold. In from the cold and the February wind, wrapped in shawl and scarf, in came Olivia.

My Olivia.

My God, even her melancholy is beautiful.

The librarian rushed to her, ministering to her, huddling close. "Over here," I wanted to shout to my wife, but that misery of a librarian scurried to block my Olivia's view. Everywhere in town, Olivia is treated with care, as if everyone actually believes her husband is far away, in grave danger at sea. As if everyone believes she is alone and pregnant.

When I saw Olivia walk toward me—or not walk toward me maybe so much as in a direction where she'd be forced to pass me—I dropped Fowles and flipped open *Techniques of Scrimshaw.* Since she now walks with her eyes downcast, she couldn't help but notice the gleam of ivory and the etched dark lines of a sea creature.

My gamble was correct. She stopped right at the children's table. Olivia knelt down by the table so as to see the gleaming scrimshaw image in the book more clearly. I stayed as still as I could manage. My wife, my Olivia, was by my side, closer than she had allowed in months.

She ran her finger over the smooth page. I held my breath as though a longed-for, long-awaited, wild animal had wandered into my yard. Any movement might scare her into flight.

Is this how the Captain felt as his schooner neared the majestic leviathan?—Had I ever loved—more to the point, had I ever really listened to the sound of my wife's breathing as I did today when she knelt on the library floor, looking at a page of scrimshaw? I wanted to quickly catch hold of her and pull her to me. Capture her. I wanted to grab her and carry her out of the library, my wife and our child, take her to our home, strip her of the linen costume, and make her again my twenty-first-century wife. Instead, I stayed still. I adjusted my breathing to hers. I edged toward what I might say that wouldn't make her flee.

"A thousand apologies. I came upon you inadvertently," I whispered. Why this is what sprung from my lips, I'm not sure. It is, in fact, what Charles says in an early chapter when he comes upon Sarah, the French Lieutenant's woman, sleeping on the rampart high on the craggy coastal cliff. I'd read the line in the CliffsNotes.

She looked at me, not so much startled as bewildered.

"A thousand apologies, Olivia," I repeated and dared then to meet her eyes. And there it was—I was sorry—not for my thousand marital mistakes, not for having hit Olivia or asking her to marry me in a graveyard, not for the bottle of whiskey that, even as I spoke, was pulled out for a fortifying nip, not for not having cherished from the first instant my boy Josiah or my bonnie Annabelle, and not for all the ways I'd fucked up, would always fuck up, even with foresight and hindsight. No, looking at my beautiful wife, my Olivia, who carried our baby, I was sorry because I could see that she recognized me, had never not recognized me, and that all of this she had always known.

Olivia did not respond. She picked up—one by one—each of the books I'd assembled. I thought she would surely be impressed with the Olmsted, and was gratified when she paused over it to read a few pages. Then she lifted from the Formica table a piece of paper I recognized as the Captain's stationery. There were his neatly penned sentences. The letter was incomplete; he always filled two pages. I wanted to grab it back from her. But I wanted to watch Olivia so close-up as she read his words. I wished she'd read it aloud. I longed to hear her close-up utter his selfless devotions, his every tenderness, and his openhearted consistency—*We have been short of provisions, dearest wife, and many aboard suffer for want of vegetables. It is in such moments I find consolation thinking of you, rosy-cheeked in winter. I wish only that I had word of your good health and happiness.* I mouthed the words as she mouthed them.

"He's a better man than I'll ever be," I said. It was less a confession than a fact we both knew.

Olivia reached and put her fingers to my face in that way of hers. She pressed a little too intently. But there it was, the flesh of my wife against my flesh. If she'd punctured my skin, I wouldn't have drawn away.

"I'll always prefer him," she said. There. What was known was now spoken between us. I was wrong, not wholly unimagined so much as wholly unpreferred.

When she stood, her hand jerked back from my face. She looked momentarily startled, then she settled both hands on the roundness of her belly. She cocked her head as if listening to something she couldn't quite understand.

"The baby?" I asked. "May I?" I reached up but stopped short of touching the cloth of her skirt. How long we stayed like that—me reaching toward the fullness of her stomach, to our child within her; Olivia looking down at where I sat in a child's chair, reaching up to her—I can't quite say.

Behind her, the librarian puffed up, eager to pounce and beat me.

"Not yet," Olivia said and turned away from my hand. Then without any rush, my wife made her bonneted way out of the god-forsaken fluorescent-lit library.

This, the end of my story: like me, it's wobbly, more often than not unable to walk a straight line. I have been away, at sea, adrift. I wish I came home bearing exotic gifts, tales of the South Seas and perils of rounding angry Cape Horn, but I never left port.

Here is what I imagine I saw. When Olivia said, "Not yet," she smiled, perhaps just the merest sliver of a smile. But because *not yet* means there will be a *yet*, a *now*, I continue.

Scrimshaw is a sailor's art, an art made of long absences, idle hours scratching at whalebone to ease the loneliness of months far from home. The gift brought home is inked with loneliness. There is little one can do if, when etching into bone, a mistake is made. If it's early, you can sand a bit, but later the only choice is to go darker with the mark. A drawn line is fine, but it's often better to stipple close, close, and closer, dots of different depths and widths to form a solid line. This also yields a more varied inked texture. It's an art of precision, but also one of commitment.

So I return to my original questions. What do we know about anyone's marriage? What do we know of our own?

I know I'm not the Captain, having neither his manners nor the strength to lead men into perilous waters through the ravages of storms. I am only what you see: stumbling drunk, public fool, not even notorious or feared. A capon. I cluck; I whine. I am mutinous. Hungry for the fast buzz, the fast return, stupid and fatted on a fatuous love of the very sordid boon that my own Wordsworth abhorred.

So be it, I'm not Wordsworth. If I've recited his poems, declaimed them on the town green, I did so with vanity, not imagination. My poet imagines the brutal force of Proteus rising or of hearing Triton's horn; at best, I hear the muddled iambic of my addicted, industrialized heart.

But I am alive. And that counts for something.

No matter how many days Olivia walks the shore road or

paces the small, flat square of the Hardwick House widow's walk, the Captain's ship will not cast a fair sight nearing the harbor; the Captain will not come home, will never walk through the low door of the Hardwick House, overjoyed to find his wife rocking the parlor cradle. Yet, despite everything that's gone on seemingly to the contrary, recall that Olivia is skeptical by nature, not quick to accept an easy offer, not easily persuaded by illusion. Yearning has its limits. This is what her smile—I am certain I saw it!—this is what her smile said. Even if I can invent him, I will never be him.

But who cares, I am alive.

Olivia, let these stippled dots connect so that you will know I love my wife. No doubt, not well, and never nearly enough. For this, and for my belief that my paltry efforts at truth have persuaded your return to this injured century, I am forever sorry, drunk, and yours.

Acknowledgments

I'd like to thank the editors at the following magazines, where some of these stories have appeared: *Bomb, Columbia : A Journal of Literature and Art, The Literarian, Noon, Ohio Review, Salmagundi, StoryQuarterly,* and *West Branch.*

My deep gratitude to Hedgebrook for a view of Rainier, the garden's bounty, a full shed of wood and the hours to work; to the writing communities of the Atlantic Center for the Arts, Fine Arts Work Center, and the New York State Writers Summer Institute; and to Davidson College for 326 Concord, where I was able to finish these stories. A special thanks to Katie Byrum. All thanks to Four Way Books' staff. And thanks always to my tribe—kids, family, friends—for joy, sustenance, wise counsel and hilarity. Some of these stories have been generously encouraged and sharpened by the intelligence and kindness of Donna Masini, Diane Williams, Robert Boyers, Bruce Van Dusen, Bill Clegg, Martha Rhodes, and Martha Carlson-Bradley.

Victoria Redel is the author of four books of fiction and three books of poetry. She teaches at Sarah Lawrence College.